"Do you think about our night together?" he asked.

Kendall waited to answer, not sure if it was better to lie and protect herself or give in to the truth. "I think you know the answer to that question."

Sawyer sat next to her on the couch. He took her hand. "I had a similar problem, but I didn't tell you. I think about everything. Asking you to dance. Having you in my arms on the dance floor. That whole night together. What that first kiss was like."

He was leaning closer, giving in inch by inch, and she mirrored his every move. Their mutual resolve was evaporating before her eyes. "It was a great one."

He rubbed the back of her hand with his thumb softly. Carefully. "One of the best."

"The kiss goodbye was pretty amazing, too," she said. "I tried to send you a message with that kiss."

"And what message was that?" He moved his head closer and nudged at her hair with his nose before pressing his lips to her cheek.

Her eyelids fluttered. He was sending electricity straight through her. "The message was you'd better call me."

"Let me send my own message."

His lips fell on hers, strong and insistent.

* * *

Pregnant by the Billionaire is part of The Locke Legacy—

This family's glamorous Manhattan hotel is a five-star location for love.

Dear Reader,

Thank you for picking up *Pregnant by the Billionaire*. I'm so excited about this book, as it's the start to The Locke Legacy series, about a huge New York family with lots of secrets, set against the backdrop of the historic family-owned hotel The Grand Legacy. Think of it as a family homestead, plopped down in the middle of Manhattan.

This first story centers on Sawyer Locke, the heir of the hotel, and Kendall Ross, the woman he hires to do his PR. They have each other's number from the very beginning, but neither wants to admit it. I really enjoy writing that "I want you, but you're bad for me" friction. It's way too much fun. Sawyer has a difficult time trusting women, and Kendall has a real wariness of wealthy, powerful men. That didn't keep them from falling into bed at a friend's wedding, though!

An unexpected pregnancy forces them to work past their fears. Kendall must accept that Sawyer isn't just another rich guy. He's worked hard to define himself outside the confines of his family, and he's had his heart broken badly. Kendall has similar demons to wrestle. Part of her wants to be like the mother she loved so much, and part is determined to keep from repeating her mother's mistakes. It's a rocky road for Kendall and Sawyer, but starting their own family ultimately becomes the most important thing. I hope you enjoy this start to the series!

Drop me a line anytime at karen@karenbooth.net. I love hearing from readers!

Karen

KAREN BOOTH

PREGNANT BY THE BILLIONAIRE

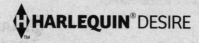

HARLEQUIN®DESIRE

ISBN-13: 978-0-373-83857-8

Pregnant by the Billionaire

HARLEQUIN®
www.Harlequin.com

Printed in U.S.A.

Karen Booth is a Midwestern girl transplanted in the South, raised on '80s music, Judy Blume and the films of John Hughes. She writes sexy big-city love stories. When she takes a break from the art of romance, she's teaching her kids about good music, honing her Southern cooking skills or sweet-talking her husband into whipping up a batch of cocktails. Find out more about Karen at karenbooth.net.

Books by Karen Booth

Harlequin Desire

That Night with the CEO
Pregnant by the Rival CEO
The CEO Daddy Next Door
The Best Man's Baby
The Ten-Day Baby Takeover

The Locke Legacy

Pregnant by the Billionaire

Visit her Author Profile page at Harlequin.com, or karenbooth.net, for more titles.

For my kids, I love you more than you'll ever know. Also, I'm sorry for the many times dinner has been late (or was pizza delivery) because I was writing. The world needs love and romance, and every time you give me a free pass, you help to make that possible. That's yet another reason to love you.

One

Sawyer Locke marched into his Manhattan office, phone pinned between his ear and shoulder. "That's your answer? You don't know how the story ended up in the paper?" He slammed the newspaper down on his desk. Grand Legacy Hotel Rebuild in Shambles. "You're my PR company. Am I not paying you to be on top of this? The reporter didn't come to you for a comment? Because she sure didn't call me."

"I don't know what to tell you, Mr. Locke. It came out of nowhere."

Nowhere. Sawyer suspected the likely origin of this story, and it didn't sit well with him at all. It never did. He left his laptop bag on his desk and wandered to his office window atop the four-story building he'd renovated when he started his real estate development firm five years ago. No high-rise for him. Too much like his dad. Down below, the trees lining the street were turning a rich shade of red impossible to ignore. He'd been staring at the trees off and on for three days now—a near match for the hair of a woman he couldn't seem to forget. He'd had his share of one-night stands, but Kendall…well, he was having a terrible time getting her out of his head.

The changing leaves also meant December would be here soon, and that meant there could be no more disruptions on the hotel renovations. A gala New Year's Eve grand reopening cannot be late or rescheduled. "I need to know what you're going to do about this. We have to fight back."

"In your case, I think it's best if we ignore it and let the story take its natural course."

For nearly a year, Sawyer had kept his frustration under wraps. There was too much money on the line, too many people watching and waiting for him to fail. Right now neither being calm nor collected was on the table. "Absolutely not. I'm not going to ignore negative publicity." Inaction was an unfamiliar notion for Sawyer. He never sat on his hands.

"Perhaps we need to make a change, Mr. Locke. Maybe we're no longer the right firm for you."

Dammit. Sawyer knew that tone, that tentative tremble in a person's voice. That was the sound of someone who'd been threatened or bought off by his father. This had happened before. It would likely happen again. "Perfect, then. You're fired."

"Mr. Locke?"

"Our retainer takes us through March. Bill me the balance and we'll be done." He hung up, stopping short of telling his now former public relations director to say hi to his dad. "Lily," Sawyer called as his brother's admin walked by his office. "Is Noah in yet?"

She leaned into view, a generous grin on her face. She was always so upbeat. "He's unpacking his things. Got stuck in traffic."

"Has he seen the paper?"

"Not sure."

"I need to speak to him. Now." He cringed at the demand in his voice. It wasn't Lily's fault everything was falling apart. "Please."

"Of course, Mr. Locke."

He stalked back to his desk and scanned the newspaper again.

Sources say Sawyer and Noah Locke are millions over budget and chronically behind schedule.

"Sources? Oh, I'll tell you the damn source," he mumbled. "And none of this is true."

Much of the Locke family is embarrassed by the hotel. Sawyer and Noah Locke are reportedly pursuing the futile project in direct opposition to their father's wishes.

An exasperated laugh rushed past his lips. Everything Sawyer did was in direct opposition to his father. He couldn't help it. They were as different as two people could be, and the more distance Sawyer tried to keep, the more his father interfered, precisely why James Locke was the most likely culprit when it came to this bad publicity. Their father had fought Sawyer and Noah every step of the way on the Grand Legacy project. Their dad wanted the hotel razed. It had been a black mark on the family name for too long. Enough was enough, he'd said. Sawyer disagreed, strongly. Luckily, the original hotel in his family's hotel empire was his. And it was nobody's call but his.

After countless arguments, the worst of which had come nearly two years ago on Christmas Day when Sawyer had made it crystal clear he was not going to back down, their father had gone silent on the subject of the Grand Legacy. He refused to speak with his son about it, and Sawyer wasn't eager to resume the conversation. Still, his father's quiet was never good. Sawyer couldn't prove it, but he was certain his dad was behind every problem they'd encountered during renovation: subcontractors not showing up, custom orders disappearing from the site. The power and water going off—more than once. It was never-ending, tiresome and costing a ridiculous amount of money.

Noah strolled into Sawyer's office, coffee cup in hand. "You rang?" Even in an expensive suit, his younger brother always looked the part of affable All-American guy, and today was no different. Tall and trim, big grin, annoyingly perfect hair. Sawyer had recently discovered a few stray grays mixed in with the dark brown that matched Noah's. At thirty-two, he was too young for that, but the struggle with his dad and the hotel was making him old before his time.

Sawyer pushed the paper across his desk. "I hate to ruin your good mood, but you have to read this."

Noah set down his cup and planted his hands on the desk, surveying the damage. "Are you kidding me?" He flipped to the back page. "These pictures are terrible. They're completely misleading. Of course the lobby is a disaster. It's the last phase of the project."

"That's what Dad does, isn't it? He's all about misleading. You know he's behind this." If only their dad wasn't several years into his marriage to his fourth wife. He tended to get bored by now, and when he didn't have "love" to distract him, he occupied himself by meddling. Sawyer would never wish for his dad to get divorced and find wife number five, but the thought had crossed his mind. "We can't let people think the hotel is a hot mess. The problem is we no longer have a PR firm. I just fired them. I'm pretty sure Dad got to them."

Noah took a seat and ran his hand through his hair. "We need publicity, Sawyer. There's no interest surrounding the reopening without it. Who's going to coordinate the media for the opening gala? Are you going to do it? I'm not going to do it."

"I hear you."

"We need to get on it today. If Dad is behind this, he's only going to escalate the closer we get to reopening."

Sawyer sat back in his chair, nodding. Their father wasn't going to let this go. He would never get over the fact that Sawyer's great-grandfather had willed the hotel to him, bypassing their dad and the family's holding company. James Locke's anger over Sawyer's control of the building went beyond what was reasonable. So much so that Sawyer was sure there was something else behind it. He'd spent much of the last fifteen years trying to figure it out, but he'd never come close to unearthing the secret. "Don't worry. I'm not about to let him stop us."

"I'd pick a PR firm myself, but you'd never let me make the call anyway."

Sawyer shrugged. "It *is* my hotel."

"Believe me. I know. If it wasn't, we wouldn't have this problem in the first place." Noah rose from his seat and knocked his knuckle on Sawyer's desk. "Do you have somebody in mind?"

Only one firm was a real possibility. "Sloan PR. They were a very close second when we started this. I made the wrong call, apparently."

"I trust you."

Noah left and Sawyer wasted no time opening his laptop and pulling up the Sloan PR website. It'd been over a year since he'd met with them and he couldn't for the life of him remember the name of the company president. Too many bits of information rolling around in his head these days…most of it not good. The site loaded and he clicked on "Our Team."

At the top of the page was a group photo of five or six people. He didn't see faces. He was too distracted by a shock of red hair. He leaned closer to the screen, squinting. Had the leaves on the trees led him to a mirage? *Is that…Kendall?* It looked like her. It really did. He scrolled down to individual photos of the team members.

There she was. Kendall Ross, Senior Director, Public Relations.

He sat back in his chair and let his eyes rest on her full ruby lips, creamy skin with hints of peach and gold, the bright blue eyes that had given him a verifiable moment of weakness on the dance floor at his friend Matt's wedding six weeks ago. She was just as stunning as he remembered. He hadn't let the memory of her improve as the nights since then had passed and he'd been craving a woman's company. Now he was really kicking himself for not calling her after he'd returned to the city. Perhaps he should've broken his rule about getting involved. Just once.

There was one unavoidable detail about the weeks since the wedding, and it was one with which he was unfamiliar. She hadn't called him either. Had she not enjoyed herself? He couldn't fathom how that could be possible. They'd spent hours pleasing each other in practically every way a man and woman could. She'd said she'd had a wonderful time. She'd even kissed him goodbye in the morning—a slow, soft and passionate kiss that lingered on his lips for hours afterward. If he closed his eyes, it was still there in his mind.

He took in a deep breath and picked up his phone to call Kendall's boss. He had to forge ahead with the task at hand. Hopefully his past with Kendall Ross wasn't about to make his visit to Sloan PR unbearably awkward.

* * *

Kendall Ross's shoulders drooped when she scanned that morning's headlines. "Of course Sawyer Locke is in the paper. The man is everywhere." She put her phone on her dresser and scrolled, reading while she zipped up her dress. One more flick of the screen and she saw the picture—Sawyer crossing the street in front of his Grand Legacy Hotel, sunglasses on, in an expensive suit, looking like he was the King of Manhattan. How could one man wield that much sexiness? It wasn't fair.

She plopped down on the bed and worked her feet into her pumps, which had been cast aside last night after she dragged her exhausted self home from work. She shouldn't let a photograph get to her, just like she should've ignored every random reminder of Sawyer that had cropped up over the last six weeks. There was the guy who rode the same morning train she did, a man she'd hardly noticed before Sawyer. Now she knew they wore the same cologne. There was the locksmith who'd worked in her office building a few weeks ago— his van parked out front. Locke and Key. Clever. Then there was the construction project that had just started down the street from her apartment. The vinyl banner for Locke and Locke went up right after the chain link fence. She walked past it every day on her way to the subway. And back.

She caught the time on her alarm clock. Five more minutes and she'd miss her train. She had to stop thinking about Sawyer, but keeping her mind off her huge mistake was not going well.

Thanks to the romantic comedy she'd watched on TV last night, she might have a fix.

She opened her closet and pulled a dusty shoe box down from the top shelf, plunked it on top of her dresser and lifted the lid. Under a stack of old photos of her mom, she found the black velvet box. Most women might keep their mother's jewelry in a place of higher importance, but Kendall had very mixed feelings about this ring.

She opened the clamshell box and there it sat—a square setting of platinum with large diamonds surrounding a blue amethyst. Kendall would never forget her mother's initial excitement at receiving it from one of her suitors, and her disappointment when she realized the lavish ring was only a gift, an expensive means of keeping her content. It had not come with a proposal.

When Kendall was a little girl, every new boyfriend her mother brought home was a new chance at having a dad. By the time she was a teenager, she knew it wasn't going to happen. Her mom had a real talent for finding men with money and power, men who wined and dined her, took her to bed, never bothering to marry her. It meant that the rent was always on time and the fridge was stocked, but they otherwise treated her mother as a pretty bauble.

Since Kendall had devoted so much energy over the years to not repeating her mom's mistakes, it made the one-night stand with Sawyer Locke that much harder to forget. Kendall made a point of being strong when it came to men. She could dismiss them with aplomb when needed.

Sawyer, however, had been the one guy for whom she had no defense. She'd let him sweet-talk her, even when she was sure it was all a line. He'd told her she was beautiful and sexy and she'd lapped up every word like she'd never had a decent compliment. And then there was their ultimate destination that night—bed. A one-night stand was not her style, but it had felt like an inevitability only a few moments into their first dance. He was commanding and powerful and even though Kendall had always sworn she'd never fall for that, she'd practically jumped at the chance with Sawyer.

The champagne hadn't helped. The first glass gave way to flirtatious glances. The second brought an answer of "yes" when he asked her to dance. It had also made her pretend that she didn't know he was from a wealthy and powerful New York family. In fact, she'd ignored all the damning knowledge she had of him—the playboy reputation, the money—even though men like Sawyer Locke had broken her mother's heart more times than she could remember.

In the weeks since the wedding, Sawyer had proven her every assumption about him to be true. He might have asked for her number and said he would call her, but he hadn't. Oldest trick in the book, a real blow to the ego, and probably for the best. Sawyer had been a mistake.

Out of the corner of her eye, she saw the clock. No time to waste, she slipped the ring onto her left hand. "Men of Manhattan, back off. I'm engaged."

Kendall made record time down her block and around the corner to the subway stop. Thundering down the stairs, she swiped her pass and clunked through the turnstile, narrowly making her train. She sat next to a gray-haired woman who was clutching her purse to her chest. Shielding her hand with her laptop bag, Kendall eyed the ring and reminded herself what she wanted it to symbolize. She didn't need anyone. She made her own future, no man required.

The heroine in the movie with the ring had been just like her—single, making stupid mistakes with men. Creating the illusion of being a taken woman served two purposes—it would be an ever-present reminder to stay on track with her career, the one thing she could truly count on, and it kept men away. That last part was a very good thing for Kendall. Men only ever approached her because she was, as her grandmother often pointed out, buxom and curvy. Sawyer Locke had undoubtedly only approached her for those reasons. It wasn't like he'd had asked her to dance because she looked smart or like she might have a sparkling personality.

She probably never should've gone to her old college roommate's wedding in the first place. That entire dream weekend in Maine was a magnifying glass on Kendall's singleness. It normally didn't bother her, but it was different being crammed into a banquet hall with her old friends, all married or in a serious relationship. Many had kids. One was already on her second husband. They had all moved forward with their lives. Kendall had, too, in her own way—building the one thing her mom had never managed to put together—a career. She needed to get back on track. Worrying about men was going to keep her running in circles.

The train arrived at her station, and she hurried along to the office of Sloan Public Relations. She'd been with the firm for nearly two years now, and was making strides. Her boss, Jillian Sloan, had said as much.

When she walked through the door, the normally bustling office was eerily quiet. Her coworkers spoke in hushed tones, ducking behind cubicles. Maureen, the receptionist, looked as though she'd seen a ghost.

"Did somebody die?" It wasn't an outlandish question. Several people had looked a little green around the gills after Jillian had lunch brought in yesterday. Never trust potato salad, or any questionable picnic foods— that was one of the many rules Kendall lived by.

"Wanda was fired."

Kendall clasped her hand over her mouth. Wanda was supposed to get the VP job. "Fired? Why? When did this happen?"

"About ten minutes ago." Maureen leaned closer and dropped her chin while casting her eyes up at Kendall. "Supposedly she had something going on with one of her clients. You know how Jillian is."

Oh, Kendall knew. Jillian was *all* about appearances. Sloan PR was a tight ship.

"If you'd been on time, you would've been here for it," Maureen continued. "Wanda's packing up her office right now. Oh, and Jillian wants to see you right away."

"Right away?" Kendall grimaced. Had she done something?

"Yes. Go."

Racing down the hall from reception, dodging a few of her coworkers, she dropped her things onto her desk. She took a deep breath, straightened her skirt and headed back to the executive wing of their floor—two corner offices with a large, central waiting area and private conference room between. Jillian's was the larger of the two offices, but they were both impressive. The second, the one that everyone had thought would become Wanda's, was empty. The door had been left open for the three months since the last VP left to start her own company, a constant reminder to everyone that the job was up for grabs, if you dazzled Jillian. Wanda's office was closed, but a long string of profanity came from behind the door. Apparently someone was not happy about having been fired, but anyone could've told her Jillian wouldn't put up with anything fishy with a client.

Jillian's assistant hung up her phone. "Oh good, Ms. Ross. Ms. Sloan is waiting for you. Go right in."

Kendall filed into her boss's office and stood waiting while Jillian tapped away at her computer. "Morning, Kendall. I'm sure you've heard. I had to let Wanda go." She turned to Kendall, her glossy chestnut-brown hair pulled back in a ponytail, probably so everyone could admire the chunky diamond studs in her ears. Jillian had worked her way up in the world and she wasn't afraid to remind people of it. "It was an unfortunate situation, but it's time for us all to move on."

Kendall wasn't about to ask for details. She could dig the truth out of one of her coworkers later. "Yes, of course."

"This could be a big opportunity for you. There's no question you're a rising star. You work hard, you have innovative ideas and you're keenly focused on our clients. You could stand to be on time more often, but we won't get into that right now."

Kendall cleared her throat and shifted her weight. "Thank you."

"Now that we've lost Wanda, you're next in line for the VP position."

Kendall stopped herself from blurting *I am?* "That's great news. Thank you."

"Don't get too excited. I'm also considering Wes. He's right behind you in the pecking order."

The bottom of Kendall's stomach dropped out. *Ugh.* Wes was her most annoying colleague, as enjoyable as a bowl of soggy cereal. He'd raised sucking up to the boss to an art form, and took so much joy in interfering with Kendall at work that she half expected him to show up one day with a villain's handlebar mustache just so he could twirl the ends. "I see."

"Show me that you're right for this job. You can start right now. I have a very important potential client waiting in the conference room. I can't tell you what the project is, though. I had to sign a nondisclosure agreement just to take the meeting. We can't say a thing, even if he doesn't hire us."

Nondisclosure? *Must be a big fish.* "Sure. Great. What can I do?"

"Win the account. I'll be there, but you'll do the heavy lifting. He doesn't want a dog and pony show. He wants to speak directly to whomever would be handling his project. He wants ideas. He wants brilliance."

"What about Wes?"

"You get our only shot." Jillian stepped out from

behind her desk, clasping Kendall's shoulder. "You've earned it. Now don't let me down."

Kendall tried to swallow, but her throat wouldn't cooperate. Nothing like walking into a pressure cooker first thing Monday morning. "I'm ready." Just to sell it, she gave Jillian two thumbs-up.

Jillian pointed to her left hand. "Are you engaged? I don't remember that ring."

Kendall hadn't fully formulated her story, but she sure as heck wasn't going to tell her boss she'd gotten the idea from a TV movie. "It was my mother's. I found it and thought I'd wear it."

"On your left ring finger?"

"Do you ever get hit on by men who you'd prefer just left you alone?"

"All the time," Jillian answered. "It can get really annoying."

"Precisely. If a man takes the time to really know me, I can tell him it's just a fashion choice. Until then, it's a great way to keep them at bay and focus on my job."

A sly smile crossed Jillian's face. "I like the way you think."

Kendall followed Jillian into the conference room, her mind a jumble...her aspirations, her career goals, being on her A game, trying to win an account she knew nothing about. She fiddled with the ring on her finger. *You've got this.*

The minute she crossed the threshold and closed the door behind her, Kendall's stomach, already unsettled like she'd chugged a bubbly soda, did a verifiable somersault. There at the end of the conference table, in a charcoal-gray suit that made her want to bite her knuckle, sat quite possibly the most handsome man she'd ever seen—precisely the man she'd been hoping to forget by putting on her mother's ring that morning. Sawyer Locke.

Two

Kendall always prepared well for meetings, but knowledge of how amazing a potential client looked without clothes was *not* the normal intel. Did Sawyer know she worked there? Was he up to something? And then there was the question she wished hadn't popped into her head at all, one she'd never ask, mostly because she wouldn't like it if he turned the tables and asked her the same thing: Why hadn't he called?

"Mr. Locke." Jillian shook hands with Sawyer. "This is Kendall Ross. She's our top PR person. If you hire us, she'll be handling the details."

Eyes trained on her, Sawyer reached for Kendall, his warm brown eyes transporting her to the not-so-distant past—a time and place where she knew every inch of his glorious body and he knew the same of her. She should've had her mind trained on wooing Sawyer as a client, not thinking about what a fantastic kisser he was. This was such unfamiliar territory, she hardly knew what to do. She only knew that she couldn't allow herself to be distracted by things like his shoulders in that suit or the neatly trimmed five-o'clock shadow along his angular jaw.

"Actually, Ms. Ross and I already know each other." Sawyer gripped her hand, all business, but it felt like he was trying to suck her in.

Kendall nearly clutched her chest with her free hand to keep her heart from failing. The handshake was far too intimate. Too much heat transferred from his big, firm, naked hand to hers. Stupid rules of polite society—touching him was putting her off her game.

"Oh, uh, yes. We do know each other." She tittered, something she would never do, especially not in a meeting. *Get it together.* "We met at a mutual friend's wedding." Kendall scanned Sawyer's face if only to figure out what in the hell he was hoping to accomplish by admitting they knew each other. Silently confronting him in this manner only created more problems, as he unflinchingly returned her gaze, eyes singularly trained on her, making her heart beat like a fish trying to flop out of a bucket to save its own life.

"We had a wonderful time. Ms. Ross showed me some of her moves." He bounced his dark brows. The corners of his mouth twitched arrogantly. "On the dance floor."

So he *was* just messing with her. *Jerk.* First he didn't call her now he was dropping innuendo in a business meeting? Easy enough for him—the handsome billionaire who didn't have his career on the line. Of course he hadn't called her after the wedding. Guys like Sawyer Locke were too cavalier with the hearts and minds of others, especially women. He probably had them lined up around the block.

"Please, Mr. Locke. Have a seat. What can we do for you today?" Kendall was desperate to steer the conversation to the professional. She sat across the table from him, turning to a fresh page on her legal pad. When she looked up, his sights were locked on her left hand. The ring. *Good. Let him look.* Kendall glanced at the setting of shimmering stones. "Oh, goodness." She straightened it.

Jillian remained standing. "I won't stay long, Mr. Locke. I know you want to talk strategy and in that instance, Kendall is your woman."

"Is that so?" Sawyer leaned back in his chair and slowly thrummed his fingers on the table.

Your woman. Why was she having such a hard time swallowing today? And had someone cranked the thermostat? "I'm good at my job, if that's what you're asking."

Sawyer flashed his killer smile—a self-assured grin to remind her that he was not only a man who knew what he wanted, he had absolutely no problem getting it. Probably the reason he hadn't called her after the wedding. She was just another in an endless string of women. "Perfect. I need to make a change with my PR. The last firm we worked with had a hard time following my lead. I'm too busy to spend my day butting heads."

Kendall shifted in her seat. Of course. Men like Sawyer didn't like it when anyone disagreed with them. "Tell me about the Grand Legacy. After the story in the *Times*, I can only assume that's what we're talking about."

"So you saw it."

"I did. I'd call it unflattering, at best." *Even if that picture of you was hot as hell.*

"Tell me how you really feel." His voice was terse, as if he had little patience for her opinion.

Kendall shrugged. "I'm telling you what I saw."

Sawyer's jaw tensed, then he cleared his throat. "Fine. You're not wrong. It was horrible. My brother and I are extremely unhappy that those photos were leaked. We've done everything we can to keep the details of our project top secret. We can't have information of any kind getting out, especially in the newspapers. It's a disaster."

"You might be creating your own problem. Keeping secrets almost never works."

"It works if you do it well. You have to understand, we're not just renovating the hotel, we're rebuilding the mystique. We have to keep the details under wraps until the grand reopening, when all will be revealed. We're going for drama. A big bang."

She shook her head and tapped her pen on the notepad. "And as a member of the general public, I know nothing. You can't assume people know the history. I don't know much about the Grand Legacy and I grew up in New Jersey. It's been closed for more than a decade.

All of that makes me disinterested. Keeping things a secret is the wrong tack to take."

"Kendall has an excellent point, Mr. Locke," Jillian said. Any other boss might've taken issue with Kendall pointing out the mistakes a potential client had made, but not Jillian. She believed in transparency, at all times, and at all costs.

"What are you suggesting?" Sawyer's annoyance was clear. "We let people see what we're doing?"

"Let me ask you this. Would you rather have someone like me open a paper to see grainy, camera-phone photos of your hotel, or would it have been better if this morning's paper had featured professional photographs, along with a story chock-full of interesting details?"

Sawyer pressed his lips together. His forehead crinkled. Kendall took great pleasure in showing him exactly how wrong he was. "I see your point."

"Publicity and building anticipation is about the careful dissemination of information, not locking it up and throwing away the key. You have to go for the slow burn, Mr. Locke. You tease. You give the people a taste of what they want. Soon you have them clamoring for more." Finally, she was hitting her stride. Even if she and Sawyer were not in agreement, at least he would know up front that she was not a "yes" woman. Not even for him.

Jillian's assistant ducked her head into the room. "I'm sorry to interrupt, Ms. Sloan, but your ten o'clock is here early."

"Coming," she answered, reaching to shake hands with Sawyer as he stood. "I'm sorry I can't stay for the whole meeting, but I have no doubt that Kendall is on the right track. You're in excellent hands with her."

"Thank you. I'm sure Ms. Ross knows exactly what to do with me."

Kendall refrained from grumbling, but she sure felt like complaining. Much to her detriment, the man had a real talent for innuendo. He returned to his seat when Jillian left. He didn't say a word. He just looked at her. As to what he might be thinking, she had no earthly idea. She only knew that if she and Sawyer were going to work together, she needed to keep them on course. A very narrow, nonsexual and never flirtatious course, especially now that they were alone.

"So? The Grand Legacy. Do we have the job?" she asked.

He nodded, not taking his eyes off her. "I have some questions."

"Of course. Whatever you need to know." She exhaled. She could do this. Her brief history with Sawyer didn't have to be an insurmountable issue. It didn't have to be an issue at all. They were both professional people and there was a job to be done.

"I want to hear more about the slow burn." He trailed his index finger on the conference table in a painfully slow circle. "It sounds promising."

"Oh. Uh. Sure. Of course."

"Then I'd like to know when exactly you got engaged."

Kendall froze. Her pulse thundered in her ears as she scrambled for an answer. It was one thing to come right out with it with her boss, but she had nothing for

Sawyer. How was she supposed to have anticipated that he'd waltz back into her life that morning and make Operation Engagement Ring infinitely more complicated?

Sawyer didn't like distractions in business meetings, nor did he like surprises. But this was no ordinary meeting, and Kendall Ross was much more than a beguiling bombshell. She was a force to be reckoned with.

"If it's all the same to you, I'd like to get back to the PR plan. Isn't that the most pressing matter?" She straightened in her seat, composed and determined.

Even with vast amounts of money on the line, Sawyer's mind couldn't keep from straying to *pressing* of another kind—namely the moment at the wedding when she pressed against him, his hand settled in the curve of her back and everything around them faded away. It wasn't like him at all to be so unfocused in a meeting. But he'd never been tested like this either.

It was one thing to run into a former conquest months or years later and see her with a date or a serious boyfriend. That he could handle. That was the cost of being the guy who not only doesn't do serious, but doesn't get within ten miles of it. But engaged? Less than two months later? Who was this guy? Where did she find him? And how had Sawyer managed to sleep with the one woman who could move on even more easily than he did? Not that he'd actually moved on from Kendall. She'd kept wandering into his thoughts, while he kept waiting for the day when she'd simply walk out.

"I suppose," he said.

"As I said, it's more effective to release information

and images on a specific, carefully planned timetable, all of it leading up to your grand reopening. The only way to control the story is to promise the press you'll give them everything they want, but on your terms."

"The slow burn." He might come to hate that phrase. It was far too sexy, especially coming from Kendall's tempting lips.

"Yes. You have to realize, most people are terrible at visualizing things. And it might seem counterintuitive, but letting them see glimpses of the hotel now will create demand for more and more until people can't stand it and they have to see it for themselves."

She was so convincing right now, she could've sold him nearly anything, even the contents of his own wallet. "I have a feeling I should've hired you from the beginning."

"Does that mean you're hiring me now?"

He laughed quietly. She not only knew how to bury his ideas while selling her own, she knew how to close the deal. He threw up his hands in mock surrender. "I don't think I have a choice. You've made a compelling case. Despite the fact that you don't seem inclined to agree with me, I appreciate your thought process. Let's do it your way." He cleared his throat. *Idiot.* "The PR. Your way."

"Well, good. That's great. Thank you. I'm happy to hear that." She smiled, bringing a beautiful blush to her cheeks. It made him want to only do things that made her smile. But then she pushed her hair behind her ear with her left hand and he was reminded that he had zero business thinking of Kendall that way.

"So. Engaged, huh? That must've happened recently. I mean, I hope it's a recent thing." Sawyer gave free passes on most personal choices—he simply wasn't judgmental. But if she had been unfaithful to someone, with him, that crossed the line. He hoped to hell she could be trusted.

"I'm not discussing my ring, Mr. Locke. We're having a business meeting. Surely you can appreciate that."

"First off, please don't call me Mr. Locke. Considering our history, I think we're past the point of calling each other by our last names."

"Okay, then, *Sawyer*." Damn, he loved hearing her say his first name. "I'm not discussing the ring. Frankly, it's none of your business."

"Ah, but it is my business. I need to know I can trust the person I'll be working with for the next three months." He hated the thought that he might come to regret his night with Kendall. He wanted to think it had been a good decision to learn how impossibly soft her skin was, or what it felt like to have her gasp in his ear when he'd brought her to her peak.

"Are you implying that I somehow deceived you?"

"We made love six weeks ago. I'd feel a lot better knowing your fiancé wasn't in the picture then. I don't pursue taken women. The thought of it makes me cringe." That much was true. He'd lived through infidelity. He'd endured that violation of trust, and he didn't take it lightly.

She pursed her lips. "Fine, then. If you must know, the ring is a very recent development in my life."

"How recent?"

"Very. But for our purposes, it's merely a reminder that we are nothing but business associates."

He'd leave it alone for now. She was putting up walls that said to back off. That was enough. "Got it."

"So, what's your timetable?"

"The reopening gala is New Year's Eve."

"It's October 7. We don't have much time."

"Indeed." Brought back to earth, Sawyer again felt the weight of the responsibilities waiting for him—dealing with the contractors, trying to see if there was a way to get through to his dad, and hoping that, somehow, Kendall Ross would ultimately be his savior and help him pull off the impossible—a flawless reopening of the Grand Legacy Hotel.

"Can you give me a tour of the hotel? I need to see it as soon as possible."

Sawyer had a ridiculous schedule tomorrow, but getting Kendall up to speed was of paramount importance. Plus, the thought of time with her sounded like a vast improvement over what would otherwise simply be more things he didn't feel like dealing with.

"Can you meet me there at ten tomorrow morning? I'll send a car to your office."

"I'm perfectly capable of taking a cab or the subway."

"I have no doubt about that."

She shook her head. "Thanks for the offer, but I'm good."

"Fine. I'm not about to argue with you."

She stood and smiled, nearly knocking the breath from his chest. It would take some time to get used to working in such close proximity to Kendall. "I'll see you tomorrow."

"Tomorrow." He shook her hand, which felt odd. Considering what had happened between them six weeks ago, his departure warranted something closer to an embrace and a kiss on the cheek.

He walked outside, relieved that the PR was now sewn up, but conflicted about everything else. He couldn't stop wondering about her fiancé—who he was, and more specifically, how he'd swept her off her feet in such a short amount of time. Judging by the rock on her hand, the guy had money. Did Sawyer know him? He really hoped not. What did he look like? What did he do? And why was this bothering him so much?

He climbed into the back of his waiting town car and pulled out his phone to call his brother. He needed to get his mind on work and off Kendall, which would be a near impossibility now that she was on the project. But the reality was she'd never called him after their night together, and judging by the cool composure she'd radiated during their meeting, she'd done it with good reason.

Starting with the ring.

Three

Kendall stepped out of a cab in front of the Grand Legacy Hotel in midtown Manhattan a few blocks from the touristy chaos of Times Square. Fall leaves fluttered down the city street, a mix of drizzle and cool wind whipped at her cheeks. From somewhere beyond the hotel entrance came a buzz of saws and clamoring of metal against metal.

She walked into the shadow of the looming building she'd seen a few times before in passing. Right now, it didn't look like much—obscured by a maze of metal scaffolding, a tall chain-link fence and a temporary facade of gray, painted plywood. Four intimidating muscle-bound men dressed in black, wearing wraparound sunglasses and earpieces stood sentry at the entrance, sending a clear message: no trespassing.

Kendall couldn't imagine anyone wanting to mess with those guys. Whoever had taken the pictures that appeared in the *Times* had risked life and limb to do so. After researching the Locke family and the hotel last night, she had to wonder if Sawyer's dad was behind that story. From where Kendall sat, the passing of the hotel to Sawyer couldn't have gone over well.

"Good morning," Kendall said to the least menacing of the security guys. "I'm here for Sawyer Locke. He's expecting me." Out of the corner of her eye, she caught a security camera panning in her direction. Sawyer was probably sitting inside behind a massive desk, a wall of TV monitors allowing him to survey his kingdom.

"Yes, ma'am. Mr. Locke is waiting for you inside. I'll walk you in." The man opened a ramshackle, temporary door and Kendall followed him into an area stacked high with building materials. "You're going to need this." He reached into a bin and pulled out a yellow construction helmet, handing it to her.

"Is this really necessary?" *I'm having a spectacular hair day.*

"Mr. Locke's orders."

"But you aren't wearing one."

"Most of us aren't, but Mr. Locke insisted you do." He opened one side of a glass double door cloaked in dirty construction paper. The hotel's revolving door was closed off with caution tape.

Kendall grumbled under her breath, putting the helmet on her head. Yellow was so not the right color for a redhead who avoided the sun at all costs. Was this Sawyer's way of getting in a dig after she'd refused to fess up about the ring? He had to know how stupid she would feel.

They walked into what she could only assume was the lobby. The floors were blanketed in a patchwork of heavy paper. Sawdust was everywhere. Her pumps were going to be filthy by the time she left. Workers milled about, and the noises that had seemed loud outside were practically deafening. Judging by everything she was seeing, the newspaper story had been correct—this project was nowhere close to completion.

"Where do I find Mr. Locke?" she called out above the noise.

"Over there," the man yelled, but then he pointed to one of the workers.

"No. I need Mr. Locke." Kendall screamed in as ladylike a fashion as possible, while scanning the room for the hunky billionaire in a killer suit.

"He's right there," he replied, annoyed.

All Kendall could see was a man in jeans, a blue flannel shirt and brown work boots crouched down in front of the elevator. The guy had a nice rear view, and he certainly had the right hair. She took a step closer and he turned, a slight but familiar smile crossing his lips. *I'll be damned.*

Sawyer straightened, wiping his hands on his jeans. Kendall was going to have to be on her A game today. Otherwise, she might die from a lethal dose of shock and handsomeness. He approached her, the sight of his shirtsleeves rolled up over his firm forearms making her heart flutter. She couldn't afford to botch the most important job of her professional life, so she'd just have to learn to look at him as if he was a normal person and hope that over time, she'd build up immunity to his face and presence. *Good luck with that.*

"Hey there," he said above the noise, raking his hands through his thick hair and knocking dust from it. "I should've told you to dress for a construction site." He eyed her while she fought the part of her that wanted him to say something nice. "Not that you don't look great. You do."

Heat trickled through her veins. What was it about him that made his kind words so much more potent than any other man's?

"Love the helmet," he continued.

"I see you aren't wearing one."

"I know what I'm doing."

"How do you know I don't know what I'm doing?"

"This is your first visit, and I have to keep you safe."

She wasn't sure she was buying it, but she had work to do. And her hair was going to be a wreck when she took the dumb thing off. "Fine. Just show me the hotel."

"There's not much to see down here. We'll just get in the way." He stepped aside as a worker carried a ladder past them. "I'll show you the grand ballroom."

He started past the elevator doors. Kendall hurried to catch up, her eyes stubbornly darting to him—that long and lean frame that looked good in, well, everything she'd ever seen him wear. And especially good wearing nothing. Sawyer in jeans was not what she'd prepared for today. Judging by his wealth and privilege, he did not strike her as a man who would get his hands dirty. It was more than a little bit sexy.

They turned down a wide hall and the construction noise faded.

"Busy morning?" she asked.

"I was going over the restoration of the metal overlays on the elevator doors. A lot of the original art deco features were lost over the years."

"I researched the hotel last night. Everything in the older photos was so grand and luxurious."

"It was once considered one of the most beautiful buildings in the city. I'd like to have it be seen that way again."

It was indeed gorgeous in the pictures, but Kendall found the history she'd dug up more interesting than the architecture—it read like a tabloid magazine, salacious tales of events that she'd thought only happened in movies. The Grand Legacy had seen mobsters roll up in Bentleys with beautiful women in mink stoles, high-stakes poker games between politicians and Hollywood elite, and New Year's Eve parties that made Times Square look like a church social.

Sawyer led them into to a large open room like a reception area, with a chandelier wrapped in plastic and five sets of double doors. Sawyer fished a large ring of keys from his pocket and unlocked one set. "I'm glad you got up to speed. Shows me you're serious about the project."

"Isn't that the appeal? The secrets of the Grand Legacy Hotel?" She followed him into the dark room.

He grinned and nodded, then flipped on the lights. "It is."

Kendall's eyes were immediately drawn upward, to

the barrel ceiling. High above them, a procession of intricate geometric patterns in white and blue glass, trimmed with gilded metal, ran the length of the room. A soft light glowed through the panes. "It looks just like it did in the pictures. It's lit from the other side, isn't it?"

"It's meant to look like moonlight is shining through, but in reality, the fourth-floor rooms are above it. It took months to clean and repair. Entire sections had fallen during the fifteen years the hotel was closed."

"Right after you inherited it."

Surprise flickered across his face. "You did do your homework. I was seventeen. I wasn't in a position to run a hotel. But I sure wasn't going to let my dad get his hands on it either."

"I was curious about that. He really thought the building should be knocked down?"

Sawyer gazed up at the ceiling, shaking his head. "He still thinks that. Can you imagine all of this, gone forever?"

Kendall admired his profile, and the way he got lost in the details. This meant a lot to him. She could hear it in his voice. "It's going to look incredible in a magazine or newspaper. We'll get a photographer in here right away."

"If you think this looks good, let me take you up to the main bar." He locked the ballroom and they traversed the reception area to a metal door. "Ladies first."

Kendall stepped into the dimly lit stairwell. "The fire stairs?"

"Only way to get there right now. They're working on the wrought-iron railings of the grand staircase."

She began to climb the concrete steps. "How far up?"

"Third floor."

"Have you been this hands-on through the entire project? Or is it just because you're behind schedule?" Sawyer was directly behind her. Was he doing what she'd been doing earlier and ogling her backside? He shouldn't be, but part of her wanted to think he was.

"I'm here all the time. There are so many tiny details and they all have to be exactly right. I spent enough time here as a kid to remember most of it. Everything else I research in my great-grandfather's records."

"Don't you have an architect to do that?"

"I take the lead. No one could possibly care about it as much as I do."

Kendall stopped on the third-floor landing. "So you're a control freak." She didn't mean it as an insult. She admired his dedication. How many men in his position cared about the details?

He reached past her to open the door. Inches apart, they faced each other. His presence resonated through her body, memories of his skin touching hers impossible to fend off. "I prefer methodical, but sure. Call me a control freak. That's how you get what you want."

She held her breath, recalling exactly how much control Sawyer had taken during their one night together—the way he'd gathered her wrists in his hands and pinned her arms to the mattress as he trailed kisses along her jaw, her neck, then across her collarbone and down the centerline of her chest...

Now she was happy for the construction helmet.

She'd save herself a tragic head injury if he continued to plant these thoughts in her head and she fainted.

They entered a service hall and found yet another door hidden away around a corner. How anyone would ever find this was beyond her. He opened it and she stepped inside, the odor of fresh paint hitting her nose. Sawyer again flipped on the lights, revealing a room that put the ballroom ceiling to shame. She had not seen this room in her research.

A long, ebony bar lined one side of the room, with leaded glass pendant fixtures pooling light on the gleaming surface. The other side had more than a dozen intimate booths, with dark leather seats and ornate black and gold metal screens separating them. In the wall at the far end of the room was a massive circular frame, tall enough to skim the ceiling and graze the floor, and just as wide. It was shrouded in paper, but sunlight filtered through at the edges.

"A window? On the front of the building?" Kendall asked. "I don't remember this."

Sawyer nodded. "It was an original feature, but it was taken out in 1919. I had it rebuilt from the first photos of the hotel."

"Why would anyone close up a window?"

"It's a bar, and it was Prohibition. The entire thing was closed up, at least from the outside. In fact, the Grand Staircase led to nothing but the third floor elevators at that time. As far as the outside world knew, this didn't exist. But if you were in the know, it was the busiest place in the entire hotel."

"A speakeasy?"

He smiled with a hint of mischief. "You know, my great-grandfather bought the hotel with money he earned from bootlegging. The speakeasy is how he found out about it in the first place."

"So that's true? The Locke family fortune came from running liquor?"

"My family comes from very humble beginnings. But my great-grandfather had big ideas." There was a fondness in his voice that warmed her heart. She hadn't expected him to be sentimental. "It makes my father crazy. He'd prefer to think of the Lockes as upper crust through and through, but that's just not the case."

"You can't change family history."

"Exactly. And isn't that the American dream? Make your way however you can? So much of what I have is because my great-grandfather was determined to make a better life for himself. Starting with this hotel."

The fire in his eyes and the way color rose in his cheeks said how much this meant to him. She'd learned in Maine exactly how passionate he could be. "I'm sensing the hotel is more than another piece of your real estate portfolio."

He turned to her, scanning her face. It was much more difficult to stay trained on the task at hand when they were alone like this. Another time or in another set of circumstances, it wouldn't take much to convince her to kiss him, to see how much of his fire he might be willing to unleash on her.

But she was stuck with the here and now. Her lips and his were never to meet again.

"The Grand Legacy is my baby. I've been in love

with this hotel since I was a kid. It's a tie to my true family history, not the version of it my dad wishes were true."

The Locke family tree was starting to come together now. "Is that why your great-grandfather left it to you? Instead of keeping it as part of Locke Hotels?" Kendall pulled out a notepad, wanting to take notes. As soon as she got back to the office, she was going to pen her first press release and start setting up the key interviews.

Sawyer shrugged. "Care to sit for a minute?"

"Oh, sure." They slid into the closest booth.

He reached across the table and took the construction helmet off her head. It was such a simple gesture, but it all happened in slow motion as it brought back a memory from the wedding. "I think you can lose this. You're safe."

She smoothed her hair, wishing she had a mirror and a moment to collect herself. She saw him in the elevator at the wedding, the moment he'd brushed the side of her face with the back of his hand, telling her she was the most beautiful woman he'd ever seen. It had probably been a line. She'd suspected it at the time. But part of her wanted so desperately to believe it, even now, when she wasn't supposed to be thinking about him like this. That was how good Sawyer was at getting what he wanted. He made her want to give him everything.

"Can I ask you a question?" she asked, steadying her voice. "Do you think your dad could be behind the story in the paper?"

Sawyer didn't say a thing, he merely melted her resolve with his warm brown eyes. They were so soulful, so deep, so sad. "I don't have proof, but yes, there's more than a chance. Is it that obvious?" His voice was low and rough.

Kendall felt no sense of victory from having made this deduction. "Things all seemed to point to him. Is he really that vindictive? You'd think he would be happy you have this project. It means so much to you. He doesn't even like the hotel, so why not just let you have it? Why would he want to hurt you like that?" She was surprised at the way her voice cracked, the way her emotions had bubbled to the surface. She was normally much more even-keeled, but her heart went out to Sawyer. She and her mom had butted heads over the years, but it was only ever out of love. They had both wanted the best for the other person. That did not appear to be the case for Sawyer.

He nodded and sat back, draping his arms across the back of the booth. "As far as he's concerned, I'm guilty of far more than inheriting the hotel. I'm guilty of defying him. He does not like it when he doesn't get what he wants." Everything in his tone was dead serious. The problems between Sawyer and his dad were much more than family squabbles.

"I see."

"Which is precisely why he's not going to stop me."

And that made Kendall want to give Sawyer every last thing she could.

Sawyer hated having to admit to Kendall that his father was his biggest problem. She might not be his to impress, but he didn't want her to see him as vulnerable. He didn't play that game. Not being able to stop or control his dad made him feel powerless, and he despised that more than anything. He knew, deep down, that it wasn't true weakness—he merely wasn't willing to stoop to his dad's level. Sawyer fought with fists up, out in the open. His dad not only wasn't afraid to deliver a sucker punch, it was his specialty.

"I'm so sorry, Sawyer. That's terrible." She reached across the table, her eyes brimming with sympathy.

At first, he took it as a sweet gesture, until he saw the ring on her finger and the air was sucked out of the room. "Pretty sad, isn't it? All of this money on the line and I'm fighting my own dad? And it's not just the newspaper story. There have been countless problems with the construction. Problems that all point to him."

"Can't you call a truce? Reason with him?"

Sawyer laughed quietly. She had this edge of hopefulness that was so appealing. Damn the guy who had to go and put that rock on her finger. If it wasn't there, he could at least take her out for a drink and apologize for not calling her. He could feel like less of an ass. "It's impossible to reason with someone when they won't own up to doing anything wrong."

She gnawed on her lip, seeming deep in thought. "Do you want to do something about that? Go on the offensive?"

"I'm not sure I know what you mean."

"The PR campaign. We can put a new twist on it. Show your dad not only that you won't be stopped, but maybe thumb your nose at him a little. I mean, if you're up for that."

"I don't want to get sneaky. It's not my style."

"Oh, this won't be sneaky. At all. There will be no doubt what we're up to."

Sawyer had been really turned on yesterday by Kendall's talk of the slow burn, but this was taking things to a whole new level. A woman with a plan to get back at his dad? If she wasn't engaged, the temptation to cross every professional boundary between them would be too much. "Please. Go on."

"Let's flaunt the history of this hotel that you love, everything your great-grandfather wasn't ashamed of, but your dad hates."

Sawyer was dying to know where she was going with this. "How, exactly?"

"We'll still show the care and time you've put into restoration. We'll show off the Grand Legacy's beauty and luxury, just as we planned, but we talk about it in the context of the scandalous things that went on. We sell the Grand Legacy as the most notorious hotel in the city."

The words rang in his head. *The most notorious hotel in the city.*

"You know how people are." Kendall furiously scribbled notes as her voice became even more animated. "They love things that are naughty. Wrap that up in a sexy, beautiful package? It's irresistible."

Sawyer had to stem the tide of blood flowing in his body right now…the sexy, beautiful woman in front of him was too much to take. Every inch of him grew taut. If he could have done anything at that moment, it would've been to kiss her, and take her—right there in that booth. He couldn't have been more attracted to her if he tried. "I love it. It's fantastic. Absolutely incredible." *You're incredible. And I'm an idiot.*

She wrote down a few more things, then flipped her notebook closed and tucked it inside her purse. "Great. Well, I think this has been very productive. I should head into the office. I want to finish fleshing out my publicity plan, start setting up interviews. We'll start right away. Jillian is going to want an update and I know you're busy."

"I can show you more the next time you're here. The restaurant is close to completion and we're opening a second bar."

"Sure. Next time."

He was going to have to fight his anticipation of next time. "Let me call a car for you."

"You don't have to do that. I'll hop in a cab."

He was still struggling with the distance she was so determined to keep between them. Sure, this was just business, but they did have a rapport. There was a spark between them—and frankly, it wasn't that unlike their dynamic at the wedding. Did she have a spark like that with her fiancé? If so, it was no wonder the guy had been smart enough to pop the question. Sawyer was once again asking himself how smart it was to be the guy who won't keep a woman around. "At least let me walk you outside and hail you a cab."

She nodded, her eyes softening. "Okay. But do I have to wear this thing?" She grabbed the yellow construction helmet from the table.

He took it, their fingers brushing. Touching her was

the final blow—he was going to need some alone time after this. "Just stay close to me."

Once outside, they stopped at the curb, both of them eyeing the street for a cab.

"I really do love your plan." He didn't want their talk to end. He was already disappointed she was leaving.

"Call my cell if you need to reach me." She cleared her throat and looked off in the distance down the street, avoiding eye contact. "You still have my number? From the wedding?"

He'd wondered when this would come up. "I do." A moment of choking silence played out.

"So you chose not to call me," she said matter-of-factly.

He didn't enjoy being the way he was with women, unable to take things beyond the very beginning; he'd merely learned to accept this as one of his shortcomings. "If it makes you feel any better, I don't call any women."

"Ever?"

"No. Sorry."

"Then why ask for her number at all? That's just classic jerky guy behavior. I would expect better of you."

Sawyer wasn't a big fan of her characterization, but he'd had a few drinks thrown in his face. Kendall wasn't the only woman with this opinion. "I suppose it is. But it's not like you called me either."

"Call me old-fashioned, but I wait for a man to call."

Yeah, Sawyer wasn't buying that. Kendall was too strong, too independent, too bullheaded. "And call me old-fashioned, but you're engaged now, so you must be happy I didn't call you." That ring on her finger was the real reason she hadn't called him. And she had no right to get angry with him for something that had worked out in her favor. "Your fiancé is probably happy about it, too."

Kendall didn't say a thing. She didn't even look at him.

"Lucky guy." Sawyer wanted to punch himself for his inability to let this go, but there was this curiosity building up inside him that refused to go away. Call it competitiveness—he had to know what the guy who landed Kendall was like. What made him so special?

"Hmm?" She cast her sights back at him for only an instant.

"Your fiancé. He's a lucky guy."

"Unless you're guessing someone's phone number, it doesn't take luck to make a call."

Ouch. "There's a cab coming." He stepped into the street and raised his hand. She was only a few feet away, not looking at him, her shoulders tense. He'd upset her. Her hair fell across her cheek, and she quickly tucked it back behind her ear. He didn't want to stare, but it was impossible to tear his vision away—she was too beautiful. Too gorgeous. Too frustrating.

The taxi stopped. He opened the door and watched as she climbed in, catching a glimpse of her long and shapely leg as her skirt hitched up. He would've done anything to climb into the backseat with her and take her to his place—make up for being the guy who hadn't called. For the first time in a really long time, he was second-guessing his well-honed talent for avoiding romance. He hadn't always been that guy. Only hurt had made him into that, hurt that could never be undone.

"Thanks for the tour." She peered up at him with her deep blue eyes.

"Thank you for your amazing ideas. I can't wait to get started. I can't wait to tell my brother."

She smiled, her face lighting up as it should have. She'd done an incredible job. "I'm glad our professional relationship works so well. Since the other never would have."

Well then. "Right. Me, too." Sawyer reluctantly said goodbye and closed the car door, wandering back to the curb, trying to shake the effects of Kendall's words—all of them. Only work would get him back on track. He dialed Noah's number.

"How'd it go with the tour?" his brother asked.

Sawyer watched as the cab turned and drove out of sight. "I think the woman might be a genius. And that means we're changing everything. We're turning the whole thing upside down."

Four

"What time is Locke coming in?" Kendall's work nemesis, Wes, sauntered into the conference room and snatched a cookie from the tray she'd set out for Sawyer.

Kendall smacked his hand. "It's *Mr.* Locke. And those cookies aren't for you."

Wes shrugged and plopped down in one of the conference room chairs. Everything about him screamed arrogance—his unmoving hair, the shine of his shoes, even the way he rocked in the chair. "I still don't understand why Jillian gave you first shot at this account. She's going to end up regretting it."

Kendall fought the urge to scream at him to leave her alone. Some day he would be her subordinate. Then she could yell if she wanted to. For now, best behavior. "I'm standing right here."

"And your point would be what?"

"I swear to God, you are the only person on the planet who bad-mouths someone to their face. Can't you be civilized and go gossip about me in the break room like a normal person?"

He wagged a finger at her. "I do not sugarcoat. You should know that by now."

"We're in PR. The whole job is sugarcoating and creating illusions."

"Is that what you're doing with that ring? Creating illusions?"

When Wes had first asked about the ring, she'd simply told him to butt out of her personal life. The next twenty times he'd asked, she'd ignored him. Apparently that wasn't a strong enough signal. "I told you before. It's none of your business."

"You're only saying that because you don't want to tell the truth. You *aren't* engaged. You're only letting people think that you are. I can't decide if it's smart or incredibly sad. Care to weigh in on it?"

The blood drained from Kendall's face, but she did her best to overlook her body's traitorous response. She wasn't going to dignify his question with an answer.

"Look. I get it," he continued. "We work for a woman who is very clear about where the lines are. I've seen clients flirt with you. So you want to send everyone a polite warning to stay away. With the VP job in play, it might be genius. If it helps you stay out of trouble and get the job."

It was one thing to have her close friends at work know the truth. She couldn't lie to them. Wes? His personality, and his agenda, made it easy to keep everything from him. "It's a lovely theory, Wes. Truly lovely. Now please leave. I have to finish preparing. You're distracting me."

"Let me stay for a few minutes. I think you should introduce me to Locke. He's our newest and biggest client. I should at least be up to speed on this project. You're not the only one with a shot at VP."

"No. You are not meeting Sawyer Locke."

"Why not?"

Kendall had had enough. "Because you're annoying the hell out of me and I have work to do." She marched over to Wes's chair and began pushing him out of the conference room, but he was much heavier than she'd guessed. She only got a few inches before he stopped her by digging his heels into the carpet.

He stood and turned, jabbing a finger at her face. "You are ridiculously territorial, Ross. I won't forget this."

Kendall shook her head. "Of course you won't. I expect nothing less of you."

Wes took a cookie, stuck it in his mouth, holding it in his teeth while he grabbed another and left.

Kendall blew out a long breath. She wasn't about to let Wes get to her any more than he already had. She took her seat and reviewed her notes. She had to focus. Everything was perfect right now. Sawyer was a very happy client, she had a brilliant PR plan and her ring had done its job. Wes wasn't going to mess that up.

Today's schedule included three different phone interviews for Sawyer to do over the next two hours. Normally, she might have a client do them on their own, but Kendall wanted to be in the room. With his dad doing suspect things and with so little time until the grand reopening of the hotel—they couldn't afford mistakes. This way, if Sawyer was unsure of something or someone asked him a leading question, Kendall could slip him a note and keep them on message.

She glanced at her watch. But where was he? Five minutes late. Not enough to make her truly nervous, but he didn't strike her as the guy who'd be anything less than punctual.

A few minutes later, Sawyer walked through the door. She looked up, noting how her immunity to his appearance still hadn't kicked in. Perhaps there was a vaccine somewhere in the world, something to prevent the shortness of breath and palpitations that came from merely looking at him. She popped up out of her seat and shook his hand, unable to ignore his steely demeanor. He was often serious, but this was something different.

"Sorry I'm late. I got waylaid in the hall by one of your coworkers. A guy named Wes?" Sawyer removed his suit jacket and tossed it over one of the chairs. "He was asking me all sorts of questions."

Oh no. "Sorry about that. Was he bothering you?" Kendall just narrowly avoided squeaking her reply.

"He had some interesting information about you." He sat in his seat and looked right at her while he rolled up his shirtsleeves, amping up her nervousness while distracting her with his forearms.

"He's the office gossip." Kendall said it as nonchalantly as possible, scribbling nonsense on her legal pad. "You'll have to tell me about it later. I think we're all ready to call in for your first interview. I've got water for you and I brought in some cookies. I don't know about you, but I can always use an afternoon pick-me-up."

"Yeah. Great. Thanks." He eyed her as he opened a bottle of water and took a swig.

One-syllable answers and a glare. Not good. "Shall we go ahead and get started? This first writer is a notorious stickler for schedules."

Sawyer nodded. "Of course. Whatever we need to do. You're in charge."

"Great." Kendall punched the number into the conference phone, still feeling like something was very, very wrong.

"I just want one thing," he said as the phone rang. "When we're done with these interviews, I want you to tell me why you lied about the ring."

The writer picked up on the line. "Hello?"

Kendall almost didn't hear what she said. She was too busy panicking over Sawyer's request.

Sawyer didn't relish the role of putting Kendall on the spot. It made the crease between her eyebrows deeper and she'd lost the warm smile she'd been wearing when he first arrived.

But he'd been lied to, and that didn't sit well with him, especially not when it came to a lie about an engagement ring. If anyone wanted to know how he became the guy who doesn't get involved, it all boiled down to an engagement ring.

Unfortunately, there was no time between interviews to talk to her about it. Each went beyond the time they'd allotted, which Sawyer wanted to take as a good sign. The writers seemed genuinely interested in the project. If only he'd shared information about it earlier, he might not be in this situation right now. Except then he also wouldn't have had a second chance to spend time with Kendall. And now that he knew the ring was a fake, he could stop tiptoeing around a few subjects.

Kendall punched the button on the speakerphone at the end of the third interview. "That went really well. You did a fantastic job. You didn't need my help at all."

"It's not hard to talk about the hotel. I could do it for hours." He'd gotten on a roll during the calls, even forgetting the topic of Kendall and the ring a few times. Now he could feel himself floating back down to earth. He couldn't work with her if he didn't know why she'd lied.

"I have a few more interviews for you to do later this week, but after seeing you in action today, I don't think we have anything to worry about. I'm working on an interview with Margaret Sharp for a week from today. She'll bring her own photographer. You might want to clear your schedule."

"*The* Margaret Sharp?" Sawyer was impressed. She wrote for dozens of high-profile magazines.

"Uh-huh. That's the one." Kendall collected her things in a hurry, like she was ready to walk out, but he couldn't let her leave.

"Don't go, Kendall. We need to talk about the ring. Wes told me it's a fake. He said he heard women in the office talking about it. He told me he even spoke to you about it." The memories of his fiancée's betrayal were right there in his head, tangled up with his anger over Kendall misleading him. And to think he'd given himself a hard time about not calling her—all of that self-torture for nothing.

"You'd believe someone you just met in the hallway over me?"

He didn't really have an answer to that. "I thought the ring was suspicious from the beginning."

"Suspicious? Why? Because it's hard to believe someone would want to marry a woman you couldn't be bothered to call?"

She was fighting back a little too hard now. "Look. I need to know that I can trust you. I can't work with someone who lies to me. So tell me now. Are you really engaged to be married?" Even though he was fairly certain the engagement wasn't real, the wait for the answer seemed unnecessarily painful. He wasn't sure what answer he was supposed to want. Either she was engaged, Wes was an imbecile and Sawyer needed to drop it. Or she'd lied and was single—a deal breaker delivered with good news.

"Fine. I'm not engaged. But I have my reasons for wearing it."

"So you did lie to me." Saying that grated on him like nothing else. He'd had to utter the same phrase to his former fiancée, Stephanie. And the answer had skewered him like few words ever had.

"I never said I was engaged. I'm absolutely certain of that. You assumed."

"Of course I assumed. You're wearing a pound of platinum and precious stones on your left ring finger."

"People wear rings on that finger. It doesn't mean they're married or engaged."

"Please don't try to talk your way out of this on a technicality."

"It's just a ring. I don't know why you're making such a big deal about it."

Anger bubbled up inside him. "It's not just a ring. It stands for something. It stands for love. And commitment." He needed to stop himself from saying more, from divulging the pain that still burned in his chest if he thought about it.

"It only stands for that if you're engaged. I never said I was."

"Fine. Then tell me why you let me believe that you were engaged."

"It was my mother's ring. It's a reminder that I need to focus on my career. Romance does not work out for me. I have a real knack for attracting the wrong guys."

"I have a hard time believing that."

She flipped her hand in his direction. "Ladies and gentlemen, allow me to present Wrong Guy Exhibit A, Sawyer Locke. He's not in it for anything more than a one-night stand. You certainly can't expect him to call you, even when he says he will."

Something about this didn't add up. "Why weren't you wearing the ring at the wedding?"

She pursed her lips tightly and cast her sights down

at the floor. She crossed her arms at her waist, as if she was shoring up her defenses. "I hadn't needed it before then."

"I don't understand. Did the wedding have something to do with it?"

"Maybe. A little."

He ran his hands through his hair. Of the many frustrating conversations he'd had with a woman, this might top them all. "I need to know what you're talking about. There are things in my past that make me very distrustful of other people." *Especially women.* "I'm putting the fate of my business in your hands. If I can't trust you, I can't work with you. It's that simple."

"You'd fire the firm?"

"I'd have to tell Jillian I can't work with you. I don't know what would happen after that."

"Oh, I'll tell you what would happen. She'd give the job to Wes, and that's not happening." She drew in a deep breath, still standing, looking down at him with her blue eyes blazing. God, he loved her fire. He might not trust her completely, but that wasn't going to stop him from admiring the hell out of her. "I started wearing the ring because you were everywhere I went when I came back to the city."

"Now I'm really confused."

"Everywhere I went, I would see a sign for your real estate company or see you in the paper. It was too many reminders of a guy who slept with me and didn't call me. It hurt, a lot. I've had way too many guys treat me like that in my life, and I had to stop repeating the pattern. I watched some silly movie on TV and the heroine did the same thing. She started wearing an engagement ring to make it easier to stay away from the guy who she knew was trouble."

"And I'm the guy who's trouble." Now his stomach was turning sour. Did she really think so little of him?

"Yes." A distinct frown broke across her face. "Look, the idea might sound dumb to you, but I had no idea you were ever going to see me wearing this ring. It wasn't meant for you, Sawyer. It was meant for me. To protect *me*." She collected her notepad and pens. "It was an unexpected bonus that the ring made it easier to keep things professional with you."

Everything Kendall had just launched at him was churning in his head. Every stupid guy mistake he'd made, the way he'd hurt a woman he didn't know well, but one he could admit to being drawn to. Her words tumbled in his head. *Wait a minute.* "What are you saying? That it would've been hard to keep things professional?"

"I'm not even sure how I'm supposed to answer that," she whispered, stepping closer. "I shouldn't even be talking about this in the office. I could get fired for this conversation. You know I'm attracted to you, Sawyer. That should be obvious. But we got it out of our systems in Maine, right?"

His heart was pounding in his chest, a reaction he didn't take lightly. What was it about Kendall that drew him in like this? What made him not want to just drop it and move on? He had to get back on his game. There was far too much evidence pointing to one conclusion—

his trust in Kendall was tenuous at best. He needed to reserve what he had for work.

"Yes. Absolutely. Out of our systems." He knew it was a lie as soon as it left his lips. He grabbed his coat and headed straight for the door, but Kendall grabbed his arm.

"Sawyer, stop. I'm sorry. I apologize. I shouldn't have let you believe what you did. That was wrong."

"I appreciate that. Thank you. Because it was wrong."

"I need to know that we're okay."

Were they okay? He needed them to be, but he was very much not okay right now. He wanted her, even when everything about being with her was messy and wrong. He wanted something that was bad for him. And that scared the hell out of him. "With work?"

"Yes. Of course."

"Yeah. We're good. I just need to go."

Five

Dim morning light from her bedroom window cast a soft beam across Kendall's lap. She sat on the bed; the ring sat on her dresser. The thing was taunting her with its sparkly brilliance. She'd been anything but brilliant when she'd decided to take life advice from a romantic comedy.

Had it worked? As Sawyer had so adeptly pointed out, absolutely not. Her charade hadn't even lasted a week. She was arguably in a far worse spot this morning than the day she'd first put on the ring. Her best defense against her attraction to Sawyer had been a ruse. There would be no more strategic straightening of the ring in front of him, sending off her warning signals that he'd better stay away. He had a much clearer path to her now. And she wasn't sure she could deny him if he chose to take it.

She'd given up what little power she had when the secret had come out, and she'd been forced to come clean with the reasons why she'd let Sawyer think she was engaged. *The ring made it easier to keep things professional with you.* She was regretting her admission like crazy, but she couldn't let Wes get her account. If that happened, she'd be done. Jillian would have her new VP, all because Kendall had chosen to put on the ring.

She was minutes away from missing her train, but she couldn't find the energy to get off the bed. It was probably just because everything at work was so ridiculously exhausting. Maybe she should make a doctor's appointment. She couldn't afford to be sick, not with so much on her plate. Still, it felt like there was a magnetic force tugging at her, encouraging her to lie back, curl up into a ball and take a nap. *What is my problem? Why am I so tired all of the time?* Maybe it was because she'd been having incredibly vivid sex dreams—her mind was probably tired from staying up all night, getting busy. She could only vaguely remember last night's, and Sawyer had made an appearance. It was one of those purely hot, unsentimental dreams where two people rip each other's clothes off and find the nearest piece of furniture. In this case, the kitchen table. *Seriously, brain? Not even the couch?*

She caught herself rubbing the tips of her fingers along her collarbone, just as she spotted the clock. *Go away, sex brain.* Time to gather what little energy she had and get on with her day.

She slipped into her pumps, grabbed her coat and lap-top bag, and rushed out the door. Outside, she was greeted with the sort of day she hated—gray and drizzling. She ducked inside her coat, gathering the collar around her neck. As she started down the street, she noticed a black, stretch limousine ahead. It was not a typical sight in her decidedly unglamorous, working-class neighborhood.

A man in dark sunglasses and a black suit stood sentry in front of the passenger window. Her mind flashed to the first day she'd gone to visit the Grand Legacy and that led to thoughts of Sawyer. Was it just that her brain wanted to go there? Or was this the universe sending signals again?

She was getting close now, and the man stepped away from the car, facing her and taking up much of the space on the sidewalk. With his sunglasses on, she couldn't read his intentions, and that made her heart panic. *What is he doing?* Refusing to slow down, she angled toward the far right-hand side of the walk, but he followed until she was blocked by trash cans. She dodged to the left and he followed just as fast. There was no path to the street. The cars along it were parked bumper-to-bumper.

"Kendall Ross?" the man asked.

"How do you know my name?"

The limousine passenger door opened. Kendall jumped back.

"Mr. Locke would like to speak with you."

Mr. Locke? Are you kidding me? Why was Sawyer on her street? Why was he sending a glorified errand boy after her? She marched over to the car, ready to give him a piece of her mind. "Sawyer, you have my phone number. What are you doing?" She leaned down and peered inside, but Sawyer wasn't sitting in the back seat. James Locke was.

Sawyer's father was handsome, she'd give him that much. His hair was salt-and-pepper, cut neatly, his face shaven. Still, he gave off this aura that Kendall knew all too well, and it was much more pronounced with the elder Locke than it was with Sawyer.

"Ms. Ross. I was hoping to speak to you."

"I'm on my way to work." Her instinct was to tell Mr. Locke that he could take his conversation and shove it, but she could only be so bold with a muscle-bound gorilla standing behind her.

"I'll give you a ride. We can chat along the way."

She could not afford to be late for work, but oddly enough, it wasn't Jillian's voice she heard in her head right now, it was her mother's. *Never get in a car with a man you don't know.* Then there was the not-small matter of everything Sawyer had said about his father. The man was known for going to great lengths to get whatever he wanted. "I don't think so, Mr. Locke, but thank you." She stepped back and turned away, but her face met the driver's chest. "Excuse me."

Mr. Locke climbed out of the car. "I want to make you an offer, Ms. Ross."

"What?" Trapped by the open car door and stuck between these two men, she was a few seconds away from screaming bloody murder.

Mr. Locke looked up and down the street. "This isn't a great neighborhood. I've heard it's not safe."

"It's fine. I like it here. I know my neighbors." The sky grew darker. Kendall had to wonder if Mr. Locke was able to summon threatening weather with his mere presence.

"A professional woman like yourself, trying to work your way up in the world, should have something nicer. Safer. More secure."

"What are you saying?"

"I have real estate all over the city, Ms. Ross. Wouldn't you love to own a luxury apartment? A building with a doorman, three times the size of your current apartment, gourmet kitchen, a concierge. No rent to worry about. All paid for. It could be yours."

This was officially the strangest interaction Kendall had ever had with anyone. "What do you want from me?"

"I understand you're working on a new project at your firm. Perhaps you could take some of my suggestions for a new PR strategy. Or provide information to interested parties."

"Suggestions? Interested parties? You're talking about your son, Mr. Locke. He's my client. I would never divulge a client's information or purposely take a third party's lead. That's absurd."

"So you want me to sweeten the pot." He swiped at his lower lip with his tongue. "The apartment and fifty thousand."

"No, thank you."

"One hundred thousand. And the apartment."

Not that she wasn't already sure he was dead serious, but this was getting scary. The lengths this man would go to get at his own son. It struck Kendall as impossibly sad. "You aren't listening to me. That's a violation of my working arrangement with your son. I could lose my job. I'm not giving up my career for an apartment or money. I'll take my chances in my neighborhood, thanks." She turned away, prepared to punch the driver in the stomach this time, but he let her past. She only got a few steps though before she heard Mr. Locke's voice again.

"You could always lose your job some other way," he called.

She whipped around, only to see him remove his sunglasses and polish them, as if they were having a normal conversation.

Kendall rushed back. "What did you just say?"

"People get fired all the time, for all sorts of things." He shrugged. "There's always somebody, somewhere, who can be paid for information. Perhaps one of your coworkers? Then you wouldn't be of much use to me or my son. I'm sure your boss wouldn't like that. Especially if it looked as though you leaked the information."

A verifiable chill ran up Kendall's spine. James Locke was evil. Pure evil. She didn't care what he was threatening her with. She'd explain everything to Jillian if something like that happened. "I see. Well, I'm sorry, but I'll have to politely decline your offer."

"There's no need to say no to anything today. Take some time to think about it." He handed over a business card and the driver closed the door, rounding the front of the car.

Kendall would've stood there, flabbergasted, if she

wasn't aware that James Locke was watching her right now. He had to think that she was nothing but sheer determination, even if she was scared out of her wits and shaking like a leaf. She threw back her head and marched down the sidewalk, all while her heart threatened to beat its way right out of her chest and the dark cloud overhead began to spit rain on her. As soon as the car passed her and turned the corner, she ducked under a shop awning, pulled out her phone and dialed Sawyer.

The line rang and rang. *Please answer. Please answer.* She got his voice mail. *This is Sawyer Locke. Leave a message.*

Short. Sweet. Not what she wanted to hear. "Sawyer, it's Kendall." Her voice trembled, half out of fear, half out of anger. Take money and business out of the equation— James and Sawyer Locke were flesh and blood. How could he treat his own son this way? It turned her stomach. "I need to talk to you right away. Please call me. Just make sure you're somewhere where you can talk. The things I need to tell you are top secret."

She hung up the phone and tucked it into her bag. Her train was long gone by now. The rain was coming down. She raced to the corner and thrust her hand into the air, just as the sky opened up. She hitched her coat up over her head, but the icy drops fell so fast they collected and dripped down her nose. Wind whipped at her cheeks. "Come on. Come on," she muttered, bobbing her head back and forth, desperately looking down the street as traffic barreled past her, every cab with its top light off—occupied. It was always impossible to catch a taxi in the city when it was raining, but she needed to get to the office ASAP and try to come up with some plausible reason why she was late. There was no way Jillian would believe what had just happened.

With every minute and every taken cab that passed, she became even more drenched and her dislike of James Locke grew—a rich man had completely ruined her day, all because he wanted her to risk everything for him. Finally, she spotted an available taxi. She practically launched herself into the middle of the street, landing in a puddle. The driver zipped up along a parked car, splashing water all over her legs. She opened the door and collapsed onto the seat. "Fifty-Seventh between Madison and Park. Closer to Park. South side of the street."

"Traffic is bad. This might take a while."

"That's fine." She sat back, water dripping from her hair onto the seat. "Take your time."

If she'd thought she was tired a half hour ago, being wet, scared senseless and feeling totally defenseless made it so much worse.

Sawyer walked out of his morning meeting with Noah and strolled down the hall to his office, checking his phone. One missed call and message. From Kendall. He couldn't help it, but his pulse bucked like a wild horse when he saw her name, even when he was still angry with her about the ring. Even when he knew damn well that she was determined to keep things professional between them and he needed to muster the same determination.

His heart felt an entirely different way when he listened to her message. There was distress in her voice and it pained him to hear it. *Top secret?* Something bad had happened. He felt it in his bones.

"I'm not to be disturbed, okay?" he asked Lily as he passed her desk. "Even if Noah says it's important, he'll have to wait."

"Of course, Mr. Locke."

Sawyer made a mental note to send Lily flowers or buy her a gift certificate for a nice night out. She was bearing the brunt of working in a very stressful environment these days. He retreated into his office and closed the door behind him, quickly dialing Kendall's number.

"Oh, thank God," Kendall blurted into the phone.

"Are you okay?" He walked to the window that looked down at the red-leaved tree. Nearly half of its foliage was gone now, most of the leaves knocked down today by the rain. Still, it had that deep, rich hue that made him think of her.

"Yeah. I'm fine," she answered, her voice heavy and weary. "No. Actually, that's not true. I'm not fine. I talked to your dad and I'm completely freaked out."

"My dad called you?"

"No. Worse. He waited for me outside my apartment this morning, Sawyer. It was scary. I'm not used to this cloak-and-dagger stuff. Your family is crazy."

Fury rose so quickly inside him that he had to keep from punching a hole in the nearest wall. It was one thing to go after him, quite another to go after a woman, waiting for her outside her home. He was overcome with a need to protect her. She never would've been in the situation at all if he hadn't hired her firm. "Where are you right now?"

"I'm in a cab on my way to the office. But I feel like we should talk about this in person."

"Do you want me to come to you?"

"Honestly? No. After what he said to me, I'm paranoid to discuss it in my own office."

Sawyer was fairly certain his own office was secure, but there were bits of information that kept finding their way to his dad. "Would you feel okay going to my apartment? We can talk. I'll have lunch brought in."

She hesitated to answer and that set him even more on edge. "Under one condition. We can't tell anyone where we're meeting."

"Why not?"

"Because my boss won't tolerate any appearance of an improper relationship with a client. If she found out I was going to your apartment, she'd flip her lid."

This was far too much like covert ops for Sawyer, but he had to find out what was going on, and he couldn't deny that if he could choose anything to do today, being alone with Kendall was his first choice. Even with the revelation of the ring, and the reminder of past betrayal it had given him, it had also brought good news—she was single. "Of course. That's no problem. I'll text you the address. I can be there in fifteen minutes. If you get there first, the doorman's name is Walter. Tell him I'm on my way. You can wait inside. He'll take good care of you."

"Great. I'll call Jillian and let her know we're meeting. I just won't specify where we're going."

Sawyer began packing up his things. "Perfect."

"One more thing."

"Yes?"

"I'm going to need some dry clothes."

Six

Walter the doorman was not welcoming. Not even close. Probably because Kendall was dripping water all over his pristine lobby.

"Mr. Locke isn't home right now." Walter's Staten Island accent was unmistakable. "Perhaps you could wait for him outside. If he really is coming like you said…" Everything in his eyes said that Kendall was nothing more than an unbalanced person who'd wandered into his domain to create problems.

"What are you implying? And I'm not going back out in that rain. I'm already soaking wet." Could anything else go wrong today? Perhaps a flock of birds could swoop in from the street and build a nest in her hair.

"It's the middle of the work day. It would be highly unusual for Mr. Locke to come home right now. And—"

he cleared his throat and straightened his jacket "—and normally, if Mr. Locke has a guest, he does not have her wait for him in the lobby."

Of course. Walter was used to seeing Sawyer with plenty of women—just not ones who deposited pools of water wherever they went. "I'm a work colleague. All I can tell you is that he's on his way."

"It's also unusual that he didn't call to tell me."

"I tried his cell. It's going straight to voice mail."

"That's unfortunate."

Kendall had had her fill of uncooperative men today. "Do I look like I'm having fun?" She threw up her hands, flinging droplets of water across the room.

He shook his head in dismay. "Fifteen minutes. You can wait for fifteen minutes. Just please don't sit on anything. Perhaps you can stand over there. In the corner."

Walter headed for the front doors. The elevator dinged. Out rushed Sawyer. "I got here as soon as I could." The flush on his cheeks gave Kendall the tiniest glimmer of hope that today might get better. He'd dropped everything to get to her. At least there was one guy on her side. "You're soaked."

"You noticed."

"So you *do* know her, Mr. Locke," Walter said.

"Yes. Of course I do."

"My apologies." He cleared his throat and pulled Sawyer aside. "She's not the first woman who's shown up on your doorstep claiming to know you."

Kendall rolled her eyes. Walter was officially *not* her favorite person.

"I'm so sorry. I should've let you know Kendall was

coming. I got a call on my way out of the office. I wasn't thinking." Sawyer raised his arm to put it around her shoulders, but clearly thought better of it and tentatively patted her on the back instead. "Come on. Let's get you upstairs." Inside the elevator, Sawyer punched a code into a keypad and pressed the button for PH. The penthouse.

Kendall couldn't ignore what her body wanted right then and there—a pair of sweats straight out of the dryer, a fluffy blanket and a cup of tea. She wanted to lean on Sawyer, have him rein her in with those long arms of his, comfort her and warm her up. She didn't want to talk. She was too tired to tell Sawyer what had happened, and now that the adrenaline of the last hour had abated, she wasn't eager to relive that rattling moment when his dad had threatened her.

The elevator came to a stop and they stepped right into his apartment. As horrible as she'd felt about flooding the lobby, she felt ten times worse now. What she could see of his private domain was pure luxury— glossy wood floors without a speck of dust, original works of art perfectly lit, expensive-looking furniture.

Sawyer took off his coat and hung it in a closet next to the front door. "Let's get you out of those wet clothes."

As if she wasn't disoriented enough, his words were straight out of their tryst in Maine. *Let's get you out of that dress.* Between his seductive lips and his capable hands, he'd had her ready to climb out of her clothes that night, but she hadn't divulged that bit of information at the time. No…she'd turned her back to him and let him unzip her, let him push the straps from her shoulder, sweep her hair to the side and kiss that spot on her neck that made it nearly impossible to remain standing.

She wasn't feeling anywhere close to that sexy right now. She stood with her arms by her side, afraid to move, lest she splash dirty New York rain all over his stunning apartment.

Sawyer reached for the lapel of her wool coat. "May I?"

He waited as she unbuttoned it. He was inches away, eyes cast down, watching. She was not only aware of every breath he took and the way his chest rose, she found her own breath falling in sync with it. This was the impossible part of working with Sawyer—sharing the same space, knowing they weren't supposed to touch. It made her pulse turn sideways in her throat, threatening to close it up. He was being so sweet right now, it only made this harder. Last button undone, she looked up at him as he lifted the heavy garment from her shoulders.

"How long were you outside?" he asked.

"I don't know. A week? You know how hard it is to catch a cab when it's raining. Your dad offered to drop me at my office, but I wasn't about to do that."

"You aren't big on accepting rides, are you?"

"Very funny."

"Probably a good move. I'm just sorry you paid such a price. I want to hear what happened, but I'm going to hang your coat up in the laundry room to dry. Two secs."

Kendall slipped off her shoes, waiting on the Persian

rug in the entry, hoping it wasn't a priceless heirloom. She was afraid to explore, even though her dress wasn't soaked like her coat. She craned her neck to see more of his apartment. It was impeccably decorated with a distinct bachelor edge—coffee-brown leather furniture in the living room straight ahead. What she could see of the dining room to her right was elegant, but not overdone—ebony wood chairs and a tasteful chandelier. There was no clutter. Nothing sentimental. Was the Locke family estate out on Long Island like this? Kendall had seen a picture of it, taken from outside the stone walls circling the property. She could only imagine what it had been like for Sawyer to grow up like that, never wanting for anything, except perhaps a father who wasn't cold as ice.

Sawyer appeared again. "Now for dry clothes." His low voice and the vision of him coming for her, all on the perfect day to fall into bed, were too much to take. Her current status of sex-obsessed tired person wasn't making this any easier. If she wanted to go anywhere in his apartment right now, it was his bed.

"That'd be great. This dress can't go in the dryer, but maybe if I hang it up, it'll be okay in an hour or two." She briefly surveyed her disheveled clothes, then peered back up at him. Now that she wasn't in heels, he seemed impossibly tall. He had a build that she found irresistible. It was as if he was encoded on her DNA—broad and lean, not a bodybuilder but muscular. She could imagine him having been slim as a boy, maybe even a bit skinny. But now he was all filled out.

"Let's find you something." He gestured for her to

follow with a nod, and she trailed him down a long hall to his bedroom. Hopefully he wasn't about to present her with clothing left behind by other women. Chances were they wouldn't fit, unless Sawyer made a habit of dating women with big busts and curvy bums. He seemed to be more of a slender-supermodel sort of guy.

They passed a number of rooms—one appeared to be his office, another a guest room. He wasn't offering details, like someone giving a tour, and she wasn't asking. Best for them to not get too involved anyway, this was already too messy. She'd crossed the line by coming here. If Jillian knew where she was, she could lose her job, no matter how innocent it might be.

Sawyer's bedroom, his inner sanctum, was as gorgeous as the rest of the apartment—inviting, but impeccable. It was on the corner of the building, with windows on two sides. Ivory walls provided a neutral backdrop for an upholstered headboard of gray wool with nailhead trim. Beautiful antique maps of the city were framed on one wall. Another wall had a large black-and-white photo of the Grand Legacy, complete with the round window on the front of the building. The bed itself was a sprawling slice of heaven, a fluffy white duvet and lots of pillows. Exactly how rude was it to crawl into someone else's bed, uninvited?

Sawyer strolled into his closet. Kendall stood just outside in front of his bureau. It was a substantial piece, possibly an antique, with a silver-framed photograph of a beautiful woman with three children clustered around her. She leaned closer. A Christmas tree was in the background, and there was Sawyer, just as skinny as she'd guessed, with a contented smile on his face.

He emerged from the closet. "I know these will be big on you, but hopefully they'll work until your dress is dry."

"Is this your mom?" she asked, pointing to the picture. "You and Noah and your sister?"

"Yep." He nodded. "Christmas morning."

"Your mom was stunning. Absolutely gorgeous." Kendall had found little information about Sawyer's mother, other than that she had passed away when he was eleven, and it had happened suddenly. The obituary contained remarkably few details.

He nodded, and for a blip of time, he seemed to get lost in the picture. "She really was. But that's my dad for you. Always with a beautiful woman on his arm."

Like father like son. "You look really happy."

"That was a long time ago." He took his sights from the picture and handed her a pair of black sweatpants and a faded red Cornell sweatshirt. "I'll show you to the guest room. There's an attached bath. Should have a hairdryer if you want to use it."

"Great. Thank you."

Sawyer led her to the room next door, which was far more feminine—a white four-poster, pale lavender duvet and a fluffy throw at the foot of the bed. "Please tell me you had a designer work on this room. It's so pretty. And completely different from the rest of the apartment."

He laughed quietly. "My aunt Fran stays here when she's over from England. She likes it this way."

"Is your aunt British?"

"No. Fran was my mom's sister. She moved overseas after my mom passed away."

Kendall could've dug deeper about Sawyer's family, but she'd been so focused on the hotel. "I had no idea."

"My sister, Charlotte, stays in this room sometimes when she's between apartments or jobs. Things are always up in the air with her, but she refuses to stay with my dad out on Long Island."

"Is it the location or the host?"

"The host. I'm not the only one my dad rubs the wrong way."

So she *hadn't* overreacted when James Locke had cornered her that morning. Kendall hugged the clothes to her chest. "You can go now. So I can get dressed."

The corners of his mouth twitched as if he was employing great effort to not smile. "Right. I should let you change."

"Seeing me naked once was enough." Why she'd had to put it that way was beyond her. Nothing like tempting fate.

"I wouldn't go so far as to say it was enough."

Kendall held her breath.

"But we're colleagues, right?" he finished.

"That's right." She poked him in the chest with her finger—another dumb mistake, no matter how much she liked touching him. "Which is why I am not here. You did *not* meet with me at your apartment."

He nodded slowly, a wide smile finally blooming across his face. "You aren't here. Never were. Never will be."

* * *

Sawyer felt like a horny teenage boy as he stood outside the guest room after Kendall had closed the door. On the other side, she was in some state of undress that was maddening to imagine. Away from the surroundings that were an endless reminder of their professional relationship, he was overcome with the realization that one night with Kendall wasn't enough. He wanted to prove to her that he was a better man than his past behavior and family tree might suggest.

He popped into his room and changed into a pair of jeans and a sweater—much more suitable attire for a cold, gray day, especially when you're spending it with a beautiful woman who has no choice but to pad around your apartment in sweats.

He put on a kettle of water to make coffee in the French press, which was ready by the time Kendall came wandering into the kitchen. Her hair was dry now, her thick waves touchable and sexy. She didn't swim in his clothes—oh no. She filled them out in a way he hadn't fully thought through—there were dips and curves and swells beneath those stretches of fabric.

"I have to say, you look spectacular in my old sweatshirt."

She blushed and gently swatted his arm. "You're terrible."

"It's the truth. You should just take it home with you. Nobody is ever going to look that good in it."

She smiled and cleared her throat. "You made coffee? You're officially my hero."

He loved that idea, especially when he felt so horrible

for what had happened that morning. "Cream? Sugar?" The question immediately struck him as unfortunate. Considering the intimate moments he and Kendall had shared, they'd never had a cup of coffee together.

"Just cream. No sugar."

"Let's talk in the living room. Might as well get comfortable."

"Yes," Kendall agreed. "I'm wiped out after this morning."

Sawyer flipped the switch for the gas fireplace as she took a spot at the end of the couch. The wind was picking up outside. It had turned into a truly nasty day. He joined her, but sat at the other end, disliking the spare cushion between them.

"So," Kendall said, hands wrapped around her mug. "I guess I should tell you why I think your dad is a total creep."

His stomach turned sour. Why couldn't they be spending time together for a happier reason? "Yes."

Sawyer braced himself for it, but Kendall didn't get far into her account of that morning's events before he was ready to blow a gasket. *The driver wouldn't let me past him. I didn't know what to do.* He'd witnessed his father's manipulation so many times—but as she said the words, as he heard the tremble in her voice and saw the frightened flashes in her eyes, images came to life in his head, and that made him even more angry.

"He offered you an apartment." That really rubbed him the wrong way. It was old-school in a bad way, like he was trying to turn Kendall into a kept woman.

"He said that my neighborhood isn't very safe. He's

not wrong, but it's in transition. You and Noah just broke ground on a project down the street."

His dad had put time and effort into researching Kendall, which made Sawyer that much more upset. Was that a thinly veiled threat in itself? His dad had some scary people working for him.

She looked down into her coffee cup, deep in thought. "Should I be worried? I mean, even more worried than I already am?"

He would've done anything to take away the strain in her voice. "No. Absolutely not. I won't let anything happen to you. I promise."

"He also offered me a hundred grand. He's desperate to stop you."

"And what did you say?"

"I told him the truth. I would never do that. That's when he threatened me. He hinted that he could make me lose my job if I didn't reconsider."

Sawyer scooted to the edge of the sofa seat and ran his hands through his hair. He didn't want Kendall to become collateral damage. He couldn't live with himself if that happened.

"I'll talk to him. This has to stop."

"Sawyer, I can't tell you what to do, but I don't think it's going to help. Whatever it is that he hates about the Grand Legacy, I don't think he's going to stop until he's sabotaged the project for good. We have some time to figure out a plan. He said he'd let me think about it. I didn't bother to argue at that point. I just got out of there."

"Then you called me?"

"As soon as he was gone. Obviously, I'm not going to think about it. I wouldn't do that to you."

A very quiet laugh left his lips, but he found none of this funny. Kendall was astounding. He couldn't believe he'd ever questioned whether he could trust her. His dad had made her an offer most people would not refuse, especially when their job and personal safety had been threatened. She was putting a lot on the line. "A lot of people would've taken the bribe."

"First, I could never betray someone like that. Second, how would I even cover that up? You'd know what had happened and then where would I be?"

"You're a smart woman. I'm sure you could think of something." Sawyer looked out the window. The rain was coming down in relentless, pulsing sheets.

Kendall picked at her fingernail. "There was a third reason, too."

"What?"

"I felt bad for you. For the fact that your relationship with your dad is so terrible."

Sawyer shook his head. "Kendall. I do not need you to feel sorry for me. You're the one who got threatened today."

She scooted across the cushion until they were sitting knee-to-knee. "Look. I never knew my dad. He left my mom when I was a baby. I always, always wanted a dad. More than anything. My mom had all of these boyfriends and I kept hoping that one of them would become my dad, but it never happened." She looked him in the eye sweetly and sighed. "I just, I realized in that moment that I'm not the only one whose dad skipped out on them."

He'd never thought of it that way. He took a moment to dive deep into her fathomless blue eyes. He wanted to get lost in them, especially now that there was no longer a matching ring on her finger. "You're right."

"I don't want to be right. Believe me. In the meantime, we need to figure out what I'm going to tell your dad. You know he's going to come after me for an answer."

His real worry was what else his dad might go after Kendall for. He had to find a way to make sure she was safe. She didn't think it was a good idea, but he might have to break the silence with his dad. He'd crossed the line today. Threatening the hotel was one thing. Kendall was quite another.

Sawyer's cell phone rang. He glanced down at it—Noah. "I'm so sorry. I should really answer this."

"Of course."

Sawyer grabbed it from the coffee table. "What's wrong?"

"Why do you assume that's why I'm calling?"

"Because lately everything has been wrong."

"Fair enough. I'm calling to let you know the power went out at the office. This storm is pretty bad. I'm going to head home."

Sawyer glanced over at Kendall, who granted him a small smile. It was probably of little consequence to her, but it made something in his chest flip. And everything below his waist flicker with warmth and recognition. "Smart. I'll work from home the rest of the day." *Stuck inside, with Kendall.*

"I'm going to take Lily with me and drop her at her place. The subway station by our office gets flooded when it's raining this hard. I'm worried she'll be stranded."

Sawyer had noticed many times the way his brother looked at Lily. He'd even spoken to him about it. Sawyer might've had times when he'd shuffled a fair number of female companions, but Noah was far worse. "Hey. Just make sure everything is aboveboard with you and Lily. She's too good at her job for us to lose her."

"You want me to let her walk to the subway?"

"No. I don't. But you could also put her in a cab."

"Good luck with that," Kendall said. "It's a nightmare trying to catch one."

"Don't worry," Noah chimed in. "I'm not about to mess things up at work by making a pass at Lily."

"Good. Let's just keep things as simple as we can right now. I'll talk to you later." Sawyer hung up, knowing he should take his own advice when it came to Kendall. Problem was, he couldn't get past the idea that their situation was different. They'd made a connection that night in Maine. Since then, she'd turned into his greatest ally in the thing that mattered most—the Grand Legacy. Of course that was an argument for keeping things professional. And that left him back at square one, horribly conflicted.

"Power's out at my office," he said.

Kendall glanced out the window. "I'm glad we're in here where it's warm and dry."

Sawyer couldn't stop his mind from going to places where he and Kendall spent the rest of the day in his bed. He had no business lecturing Noah in one breath about inappropriate behavior, when all he could think about right now was touching Kendall, kissing her, getting her out of that sweatshirt.

"Let's keep it that way. I think you should stay." *Smooth, Sawyer. Real smooth.* "I mean you're welcome to stay for as long as you like. With the weather so terrible." It was the gentlemanly thing to do. Accompanied by less-than-gentlemanly thoughts.

"I told Jillian I'd likely be away from the office all day. I told her we were at the hotel. I figured that was as safe a story as anything. It's not like she'd really have a way to follow up on me aside from calling my cell."

Sawyer nodded. "If it's okay with you, I'm going to duck into my home office for a bit to check email." *I need to cool off.*

Kendall got up. "I'll get my laptop and hang out in front of the fire. I'll need the Wi-Fi password, though."

Sawyer smiled. "It's the number *1* then *legacy*, all lowercase."

"Ah. One legacy. The Grand Legacy. I get it." She grinned wide, further chipping away his resolve.

He left her and trailed back to his office. His stomach turned when he opened his email and started a new message to his dad. They hadn't spoken in ages. The rift over the Grand Legacy was that wide.

Dad,

We need to talk some things out. I'd prefer we do it in person, but if you're only willing to do it over the phone, that will have to do. Your interference in the Grand Legacy is one thing, but you crossed the line trying to bribe my PR person, and I can't ignore it. If you so much as touch a hair on her head or threaten her job in any way...

He stopped typing. A few sentences in, and his anger was already boiling over. He had to rein it in. Maybe Kendall was right. Maybe going after his dad wasn't a good idea. He didn't want to provoke him, especially if there was any chance that Kendall might end up on the receiving end. He needed to speak to his dad in person, where he could gauge the situation and his reactions, and hopefully get him to back off once and for all. In the meantime, it was Sawyer's first priority to keep Kendall as safe as he could.

He went through the new messages in his inbox, but didn't bother answering anything that wasn't critical. It was too hard to focus with Kendall in the other room. An argument could be made that a good host would check on his guest, and that was exactly what he would do.

When he rounded the corner into the living room, he came to a stop. Before him was a vision that stole his breath away. Kendall was asleep on the couch, curled up under the throw blanket, her laptop on the coffee table. She was so peaceful and perfect—her russet hair curled under her chin, her lips the color of cherry blossoms in spring.

He was struck again by the realization that had been brewing for weeks now, clicking into place today. He'd made a big mistake when he hadn't called her after their one night together, when he hadn't let her know that it had indeed meant something to him. She'd left more than an impression, she'd left an indelible mark on his soul, one that couldn't be ignored no matter how hard he tried. He wanted to make her his again, but he didn't want to wait months, until they were no longer working together. Some other guy could come along during that time. Today might be his only opportunity to show her how much he wanted a second chance, when they could both have the security of knowing that no one would ever have to find out.

Seven

Kendall's consciousness began climbing out of sleep, but she didn't open her eyes—not yet. She wanted just a few more luxurious moments of her dream. It had just gotten to the good part. Sawyer had taken off her clothes, she'd taken off his and they were doing a perfect job of turning the sheets on his bed into a beautiful, tangled mess. It was such a lovely thought…such a wonderful idea…and if she couldn't have Sawyer in real life, at least he was starring in her dreams.

She bemoaned the thought of leaving behind such amazing visions, but she had to get up before Sawyer walked in. It was already embarrassing enough that she'd fallen asleep on his couch. She opened her eyes slowly and pushed herself to sitting. The fire was still blazing, giving off heat. There was music playing softly.

She rubbed her eyes and looked outside again. What was earlier only rain had turned to sleet. There was a glaze accumulating on the window ledge.

Sawyer poked his head into the room. "Look who's up."

Embarrassment sent heat rushing to the surface of her cheeks. "I don't know what's wrong with me. I've been so tired lately. I'm so sorry I fell asleep on your couch."

"The question is, do you feel better now? You clearly needed it."

She smiled. "I do feel better. Thank you."

"You're probably working too hard."

"Yeah. I guess."

He stood before her, hands in the back pockets of his jeans. They fit just right—not tight, not baggy. Just enough for her to recall exactly how much she loved his legs. His gray sweater complemented his eyes so perfectly—it made them impossibly dark and rich. She wanted to climb inside that sweater and get lost in it. Possibly never come out.

"I should probably go. I've already taken up half of your day. And I don't want to risk the weather getting worse." She began to fold the blanket.

"Don't go. I want you to stay." He looked down at the floor and then back up at her. He cleared his throat. "There are some things I want to say to you. Things I can't say when we're working."

Her pulse immediately picked up—between his words and the tone of his voice, it was the only logical response. "Okay. Is this about your dad?"

"No. Absolutely not." He stepped closer and crouched down in front of her. "First off, I have a confession. I watched you sleep."

Now the erratic heartbeat was accompanied by the triumphant return of embarrassment. "You did?"

"How could I not? You're so beautiful."

A compliment from Sawyer felt special, like an amplified version of something a regular guy might say. "That's very sweet. You're not half bad yourself, you know."

He laughed and dropped his head, causing his dark brown hair to flop over. When he looked back up at her, she was so quickly caught up in his gaze. It was like a magnetic lure, drawing her to look at him, and only him. "Can I ask you something?"

If it's whether or not I remember which direction your bedroom is, yes. "Of course."

"Do you think about our night together?"

She waited to answer, not sure if it was better to lie and protect herself or give in to the truth because he was clearly baring his soul to her right now. The dream she'd just had wasn't making it any easier. "I think you know the answer to that question."

"You mean the ring."

"I wore it because I couldn't forget you." It felt good to allow herself to be vulnerable with Sawyer, to let down her defenses.

He straightened and sat next to her on the couch. He took her hand. She loved seeing his fingers wrapped around hers. It was excitement and contentment rolled up in a single gesture. She couldn't deny that she felt safe with Sawyer. He was protective. She loved that in a man, as old-fashioned as it might be. She'd never had that in her life.

"I had a similar problem, but I didn't tell you," he said, seeming a bit embarrassed. "There's this tree across the street from my office. The leaves started to change the day I got back from the wedding. I swear they turned the exact same color as your hair. I would stand at my window and stare at that tree."

Goose bumps popped up on her forearms, steadily marching across her skin. It wasn't just her. "And what did you think about when you were staring out the window?"

"Everything. Asking you to dance. Having you in my arms on the dance floor. That whole night together. What that first kiss was like."

She gnawed on her lower lip, just looking at his mouth. He was leaning closer, giving in inch by inch, and she mirrored his every move. Their mutual resolve was evaporating before her very eyes. "It was a great one."

He rubbed the back of her hand with his thumb, softly. Carefully. "One of the best."

"The kiss goodbye was pretty amazing, too," she said. "I tried to send you a message with that kiss."

"And what message was that?" He moved his head closer and nudged at her hair with his nose before pressing his lips to her cheek.

Her eyelids fluttered. He was sending electricity straight through her. "The message was you'd better call me."

"Now I officially feel like a cad. I will never not call you again." He laughed quietly, then got serious again. "Let me send my own message." His lips fell on hers, strong and insistent. His hands slipped around her neck and he cradled her face, lifting it to his. The kiss was warm and wet, his tongue winding with hers. The utter relief of it set free a chorus of jubilation in her body. She couldn't believe she'd lived through two months without this. With every passionate move of his lips, she was reminded why it had been so hard to forget Sawyer. It wasn't the clues the world was leaving her that had haunted her. It was her hunger for him.

He slipped his hands under her sweatshirt, circling her waist with his arms. That first hit of his warm palms against her bare skin was enough to make her lightheaded. She scrambled to get him out of his sweater, lifting the hem. He sat back, crossed his arms and lifted it over his head. Her memory of his incredible chest was put to shame—she hadn't captured every well-defined contour, the way his shoulders stood straight, and she definitely hadn't noticed the narrow scar that trailed from his collarbone to just shy of his armpit.

"Sawyer," she muttered. "How did I not see this before?"

"It was pretty dark in my hotel room. And you left very early in the morning."

This was true. She'd also been swept away by him that night. Certainly she'd missed some captivating details of his physique. "What happened to you?" She pressed her fingers to it gently, the skin slightly raised and dark pink against his otherwise tan skin.

"Injury from the navy. It's nothing."

"You were in the military?"

"Yes." He kissed her cheek, her jaw, her neck. "Is this really what you want to talk about right now?"

It wasn't, but she tucked it away in her head as one of the many things about Sawyer that surprised her. "Will you tell me about it later?"

"Right now I will literally agree to anything you ask me." He pulled her hair back from her neck and kissed the stretch of skin beneath her ear, sending tingles through her body, making her shoulders rise up in anticipation. He took his time, and her eyes drifted shut as she allowed herself to get lost in the sensation. She tugged on his shoulders, wanting him closer, and his lips traveled back along her jaw until he finally claimed her mouth again.

His hands roved under the sweatshirt a second time, but this time he traveled north, lifting it. "I need to see you," he said, his voice low and gruff.

She smiled—whatever the cost might be later, knowing Sawyer wanted her was the best feeling—Christmas morning and a winning lottery ticket rolled into one.

He groaned softly when the sweatshirt was gone. She might have been a bit unkempt on the outside, but her underpinnings were always on point—a dark purple bra with black lace along the sides and cups. Sawyer wasted little time reaching back and unhooking it. Kendall shrugged it from her arms.

She'd had men show great enthusiasm for her breasts, but Sawyer's appreciation was different. The look in his eyes was more than lust or desire, it was adoration and admiration. He took them into his hands gently, kissing each one tenderly before he wound his tongue around one of her nipples. The skin instantly drew hard and taut, and Kendall watched as his eyes flashed up at her. The look said that he wanted her more than anything.

His lips were heavenly on her skin, but she had to have the rest of him, and the couch wasn't cutting it. "Can we go into your bedroom?"

"Yes. Of course. I'm sorry. I got a little carried away."

He took her hand and led her down the hall, but they only got halfway before he pulled her into his arms and kissed her again. They bumped into the wall on one side of the hall, turning in circles on their way into his room, her bare back brushing up against the door frame. Kendall had to pirouette on her tiptoes to keep up with him, but she dedicated herself to it. It was too hot. Too sexy.

They arrived in his room and she immediately went for the button and zipper on his jeans, pressing her chest against his and claiming another kiss. His pants slumped to the floor and she molded her hand around his length, feeling how perfectly primed he was for her. He groaned and reached down for the edge of the duvet, tearing it back, sending a few pillows flying. He sat on the edge of the bed, and tugged her to him so she was standing between his knees. He shimmied the sweatpants past her hips, then smiled and dragged a finger across the edge of the fancy purple-and-black panties that matched her bra. His lips skimmed over her stomach as he slipped his thumbs beneath the waistband and tugged them down.

"You are so sexy, Kendall. Again, I'm wondering

what in the hell I was thinking." He looked right at her when he spoke and she got the message. He was sorry. He was really, really sorry.

She was about to counter that they'd both been stupid, when his fingers trailed from her knee along her inner thigh. The anticipation crept along her skin, knowing where he was headed, and she reflexively arched into him when he found her apex and began to tease her with soft circles and the tips of his fingers.

Her eyes fluttered shut as his touch became stronger and faster. It felt so good to experience these things she'd been fantasizing about, dreaming about, with Sawyer. It was only their second time together and he'd already figured her out. He knew exactly how to touch her, where and when to kiss her. She dropped to her knees and pulled Sawyer's black boxers from his hips. She took his firm erection in hand, watching the look on his face, and the way his mouth went slack as she took strong strokes.

He had both hands planted on the mattress, looking down at her with eyes heavy with desire. "I have to have you, Kendall. Now."

She climbed up onto the bed, stretching out on the mattress, and enjoying the cool, crisp sheets. Sawyer had her so overheated, every second waiting to have him inside her felt like an eternity. Hopefully he'd remember that they'd had the birth control talk in Maine—she was on the pill, they'd both been tested. "Don't make me wait, Sawyer."

"I won't." He descended on her, kissing her stomach and continuing along the center of her chest before planting his mouth on hers. He positioned himself between her legs and she welcomed him, relishing that moment when he filled her perfectly and they began to move together. He lowered his head and kissed her collarbone. She dragged her hands up and down his muscled back, then rounded over the top of his strong shoulders and flat across his heavenly chest.

Every thrust Sawyer took was careful and deep. The pressure built quickly under its own inertia, so much so that Kendall felt like she was holding on for dear life. Finally, it rolled through her in an overwhelming rush of heat and relief of tension. She gasped his name in a single breath, wrapping her legs around his waist. Sawyer followed, his body rigid in pleasure before he collapsed against her chest and kissed her collarbone.

She found herself oddly thankful for the disastrous turn her morning had taken. If it hadn't all gone wrong, she never would've ended up tucked away in Sawyer's apartment, making love to the man she'd tried so hard to forget.

Sawyer sank back on the bed, his mind mercifully devoid of a single complicated thought. Kendall was amazing—gorgeous, sexy, smart, determined. That wasn't complicated. It was simple.

She smiled and rolled to her side, scooting up alongside him. Her fingers delicately traced his scar. It always felt strange when anything rubbed against it—a mix of numbness and sensitivity. "Do you want to tell me what happened?"

He didn't think about that day often. He'd worked

hard to banish it from his mind. It was the start of a series of horrible events that had left far more than his collarbone and chest scarred. "I was stationed in the Middle East. Peacekeeping. We were ambushed and I had to fight off a guy in hand-to-hand combat. He had a knife."

"You must've been terrified. Were you discharged because of it?"

"I was, but I shouldn't have been. It wasn't life threatening. But I made the mistake of calling Noah and he called my dad and the next thing I knew I was being shipped home. My dad pulled strings. Which I absolutely didn't want him to do. But it was too late."

"Didn't you want to come back to see your family?"

"I wanted to do what I'd signed up for, but that's not how it happened." He looked into her eyes, which were so open, taking in every word he said. He loved how keenly focused she was. "But to answer your question, I did have people I wanted to see when I got home."

Kendall's pupils opened wide. "Was there a woman waiting for you?"

That edge of glee in her voice nearly matched the anticipation he'd felt about seeing Stephanie when he'd learned he was being sent home. But then he got the call from Noah just as he was about to get on the plane. *I ran into Stephanie. She wasn't wearing the ring you gave her. She's wearing a different engagement ring. Something is up.* Oh, something was definitely up. And it had torn him up far worse than a man with a knife. "There was, but it didn't work out."

"Oh. I'm sorry."

"Ancient history at this point." Time had helped to dull the pain. "What about you? Surely you must have left a long trail of broken hearts along the way. I mean, before the fake engagement ring."

"We aren't talking about me, Sawyer. We're talking about you."

Way to deflect, Kendall.

"Plus, I want to know why you went into the military," she continued. "Is that a family thing?"

Sawyer laughed quietly. "No. It's not a Locke thing, at all. My dad went to a military boarding school, but that's not even close to being the same. I come from a long line of men who liked to drink, smoke cigars and play poker."

"And make lots and lots of money."

"Yes." He had given in to that aspect of the family history, that much was true, but it was always the Grand Legacy that was driving that. If anyone had asked teenaged Sawyer if he was going to go into the family business, he would've said absolutely not. Then he inherited the hotel and everything changed. "My dad actually begged me not to join the military. He'd assumed I'd want to work alongside him when I got out of college, but I never saw myself doing that."

"Why not?"

He shrugged. "I didn't want to spend my days beating my head against a wall. My father and I have had a difficult relationship ever since my mom passed away."

Kendall's brow furrowed and she shifted closer to him. "I'm so sorry about your mom. I lost my mom in my early twenties. It's so hard."

Finally, she'd shared a piece of herself. It felt as though a locked door had been opened a sliver. He was so eager to walk through it and learn more. "Were you close?"

"We were. Incredibly close. It was always just the two of us, so we had to lean on each other. My dad took off when I was a baby. They were young. Probably too young to be having kids."

"Did your mom ever remarry?"

Kendall shook her head. "No, but she wanted to. She really wanted to. She had a real talent for finding the wrong guys. Guys who never wanted to commit. It wasn't all bad, though. There were a lot of years when those guys were the reason there was food on the table. My mom always had a hard time holding down a job."

"It can't be easy being a single mom."

"It isn't, but there was more to it than that. I think she always underestimated herself. She thought she couldn't do much, so she'd take jobs that didn't challenge her or keep her interest, and she'd end up getting frustrated and doing something to get herself fired. It was a self-fulfilling prophecy. She always blamed herself, but I really think that if she'd believed in herself and pushed for something bigger, she would've been much happier."

"So that's where you get your drive from?"

"If you're asking if there's a part of me that doesn't want to make the same mistakes my mom made, the answer is an unequivocal yes."

He and Kendall were cut from the same cloth, working hard to not repeat the mistakes their parents had made. No wonder he was so drawn to her. He just hadn't known that particular reason when they were in Maine at the wedding. Now that they were learning these things about each other, they weren't in a position to pursue it, at least not now. Kendall's job clearly meant a great deal to her. She almost seemed defined by it. "My dad's on wife number four. I definitely don't want to go down that path. My dad practically has the minister on speed dial."

"Four wives makes me think your dad doesn't like to be alone."

"He doesn't. He's a serial monogamist. It makes me a little crazy to be honest."

"Why?"

"Because a person should learn to stand on their own before they get into a relationship. I don't think my dad has ever stood on his own. Ever. He inherited his money, his business, an important name. He hasn't worked for things."

"Not like you have."

"I'm not trying to build myself up here. I'm just saying it's one of many reasons my dad and I don't see eye-to-eye."

"Well, you definitely aren't like your dad from what I can see. Not at all."

"Good."

Kendall rolled to her stomach, lazily stroking the sheets with her fingers. He couldn't take his eyes off her—what had made him think that the second time would be enough? Where had he even come up with that idea? He had absolutely no clue, he only knew that his gut was telling him that it was going to be torture to work with her and not touch her. He might have made things worse for himself by making love to her, but there was no taking it back now. And he wouldn't have wanted to if he could.

"Are you hungry?" he asked.

"Starving. Absolutely starving."

Judging by the way the rain was still battering the windows, going out probably wasn't a good idea. He wasn't much of a cook and there was never much food in the house anyway. He ended up making a sandwich most nights or his housekeeper would leave a few meals in the refrigerator. "Chinese? There's a place around the corner. They never close. There could be seven feet of snow on the ground and the owner would still send one of her sons out to deliver."

"Sounds like Chinese then." A tentative smile came to her lips. "I should probably get dressed."

"Are you okay? You know. With the fact that we made love, and we'd said we were going to keep things solely professional?" He almost couldn't believe the words were his own. It wasn't like him to open a can of worms with a woman. It was the sort of question that could illicit hours of conversation and an analysis of the state of things. It wasn't that he didn't care with most women…it was just that he knew not to start things he wasn't prepared to finish.

She rolled to her back and sat up, tugging the sheets along with her and covering up. That single act seemed to tell more than anything. If he was skittish about being open with someone, she might be even more so. "It's hard to feel good about crossing the line. I can't lie to you about that."

He nodded. "I get it. I don't mix business with pleasure. Too many potential problems."

"Maybe we just needed to get each other out of our systems. Too many unresolved feelings about phone calls and things like that." Did she really think that? Was he the one who was going to have a hard time going without more?

"We have a good working relationship. That won't change."

"Better than good. It's great."

"Of course you say that. I pretty much do everything you tell me to."

She smiled and scooted up in the bed, leaning back against the pillows. "You are a highly intelligent man. Only someone as smart as yourself can see how wise it is to defer to my brilliant ideas."

"True. I am smart."

She reached over and smacked him on the leg. "Are you going to order that food? Or do I have to do it myself?"

"I'll do it. I'll take care of everything."

Eight

Kendall woke to the sound of Sawyer snoring and a strong sense of dread. They'd shared a magnificent evening, they fit together perfectly, but today was back to reality. Back to work. Back to having a job with a boss who didn't put up with this sort of thing. Plus, Sawyer's dad had threatened Kendall yesterday—that didn't bode well for a continuation of whatever it was that she and Sawyer were doing.

She tiptoed into the guest room and fetched her dress, which was finally dry. She wormed her way into it and zipped it up, then folded Sawyer's sweatshirt neatly. It really belonged in a laundry hamper, but she had no idea where that was and this was as good a stalling technique as anything. The truth was that she didn't want to leave. She'd enjoyed her time with Sawyer so much. Being with him was like being presented with an enormous hot fudge sundae and being told you could eat the whole thing and not gain an ounce. Mouthwatering. Delicious. He satisfied her sweet tooth. But they'd both agreed that sex and work do not mix. She could not go around eating hot fudge sundaes whenever she wanted.

She wandered into his kitchen and made a pot of coffee. Maybe a warm cup of morning courage would help soften the blow of the words that had to be said before she left. He took it with a splash of cream, no sugar. And that was exactly how she made it for him. Then she walked back down that long hall, past the guest room and his office, and back into his bedroom.

The sight was almost too much to bear. He was asleep on his stomach, the sheet draped across him at his waist. His face was turned away from her, toward the side of the bed she'd slept on. This was a good thing. He was painfully adorable with his eyes closed. She placed the coffee cup on his bedside table, stepped back and cleared her throat. Several moments ticked by. He didn't stir.

"Sawyer," she whispered. "Are you awake?" No answer. She crossed her arms, twisted her lips and looked around the room. Now what? No more whispering, that was for sure. "Sawyer, I need to go."

He raised his head and turned to her, eyes half-open. "What? Did you say something?"

Oh good God, he was even more adorable than she'd prepared herself for, especially with a crease across his cheek. Best to do this quick. "I have to go. I can't be into the office late and I really need to get home and change my clothes."

He flipped to his back, tucking the sheet underneath his body, leaving himself barely covered at all. "I hate to see you go, but I understand." He glanced over at the nightstand. "Is this for me?" He moved over on the mattress and patted the spot next to him. She didn't accept the invitation. "Wow. What a treat. Sometimes the housekeeper brings me coffee, but I'm not hot for her like I am for you." He took a sip and bobbed his eyebrows at her. "Come here for a sec."

"I should really go. It doesn't look good for the woman who wants the VP job to be late."

"Just a second. I promise. No funny business."

She knew very well that the minute she sat down on the edge of his bed, she was going to want to kiss him. She was going to want to fall back into everything they had done together yesterday and last night. That was a fantasy world worth visiting, but not a place to live. She had to remind herself of that. "Just a second." She perched on the edge of the bed and crossed her legs, trying to keep to herself, but the first thing he did was take her hand.

"I just want to tell you that yesterday was amazing. I'm an idiot for not calling after the wedding. And I'm very sorry."

"It's okay. You've already apologized. I lied to you about the ring. We're more than even on the topic of making mistakes."

"Look, I'm apologizing on selfish grounds here. I still feel like I have things to make up for. I haven't taken you out to eat for a proper dinner. If any woman deserves to be wined and dined, it's you." He cleared his throat and sat up in bed.

Kendall closed her eyes. It was one thing for him to tempt her with his body, but quite another for him to pursue her with his words. She had no defense for a man who could say romantic things. She had to remember how often those words ended up being empty, holding nothing real. "Maybe a work dinner. Maybe. Definitely no wining and dining. Not while I'm working for you. And we're going to have to talk about this another time. I'm going to be late."

"Tonight?"

She blinked about fifty times. "You do remember what a risk I took by coming over here, don't you? By staying over here? By sleeping with you. This can't happen again. It was wonderful, but it can't happen again."

He narrowed his gaze and a crease formed between his eyes. "I took a risk, too. What if something bad happened between us? I would still need your help on the Grand Legacy. And then where would we be? Stuck in an uncomfortable working situation, and I don't have time for that."

Kendall couldn't even believe what he was saying. He'd taken a risk? She got up from the bed and straightened her dress, making a point of standing back so he couldn't touch her. "Perhaps you took a risk, too, but I took a far greater one. You are your own boss. The worst thing you'll have to endure is a few awkward conversations. I am not my own boss. I do not have the safety net of a trust fund or a vast inheritance or even actual job security. My boss would fire me, no questions asked, if she knew about this."

"How in the world is anyone going to find out? It's not like we weren't careful."

"Sawyer, listen to yourself. Your dad is watching your every move. And I'm fairly certain after yesterday that he's following mine, too. I'm the one who has to walk downstairs right now and get into a cab. Anyone could see me leaving your apartment building. And then what?"

Sawyer sighed and absentmindedly scratched a spot right above his belly button, where an inexplicably sexy trail of hair led both north and south. It'd be a miracle if she got out of Sawyer Locke's apartment alive. "I'd like to see you again."

"And you will. When we meet at the hotel the day after tomorrow for the Margaret Sharp interview. We'll see each other and our working relationship will remain in good condition, we'll get some fabulous photographs of your beautiful hotel and come New Year's Eve, your hotel will reopen to so much fanfare your head will be spinning."

"That's not what I meant."

"But that's what's most important to you, isn't it? The hotel?"

"That's not a fair question. We don't know each other that well."

"Exactly the reason neither one of us should risk everything, just because we enjoy having sex with each other."

"You certainly know how to be the voice of reason,

don't you?" He climbed out of bed, forgoing the sheet, walking up to her stark naked. "Just promise me one thing."

Kendall felt like her heart was about to throw in the towel as he crept closer. How could it withstand the stops and starts involved with being around Sawyer? And then there were her poor eyes…she knew she should be looking at his face, but it was hard not to take one last look at everything she was giving up. "What's that?"

He grasped her elbow and leaned into her. "On New Year's Eve, when you've done your job, and my long nightmare is over, tell me you'll kiss me when the clock strikes twelve."

Kendall knew his request would eventually prove to be an empty statement. Sawyer was experiencing some sort of sex-induced amnesia. He didn't date. He didn't wait around for women. By the time New Year's Eve arrived, he'd have some other woman on his arm and Kendall would be forced to smile and pretend like it didn't bother her. But that would only last one night and she could probably live through that.

"Okay. I promise." She let herself out of his apartment and hurried downstairs to the lobby, but she was now faced with Walter, while she was essentially doing the walk of shame in yesterday's rumpled dress.

"Yes, of course," Walter replied when she asked him to hail her a cab, but Kendall could read the disapproving tone of his voice.

She put on her sunglasses and didn't say another

word as Walter walked out to the street and blew a whistle when a cab slowed at the intersection.

"Thank you," she said, slipping a few dollars into Walter's hand. She ducked into the cab and closed the door right away. They were only partway down the block when her phone beeped with a text from Wes.

What happened to you yesterday?

She could already tell today was going to take great amounts of patience. Grand Legacy. Lots to do. Weather didn't help.

Were you with Sawyer?

Kendall's focus narrowed on her phone. Was she becoming overly paranoid? Yes. At the hotel.

She didn't enjoy lying, but Wes was a special case in her mind. His behavior begged for selective information. Luckily, he stopped the inquisition there. Kendall slumped back in the seat, feeling as conflicted as she'd ever felt. Yesterday and last night with Sawyer had been everything she could have wanted from a night with him. But more of that wasn't in the cards for her right now. No use getting all excited about something that wouldn't last, however enjoyable and tempting it might be.

Kendall asked the driver to wait for her when she got to her apartment. She ran inside, changed clothes, sprayed some dry shampoo in her hair and was back in the cab in ten minutes flat. Balancing her cosmetic bag on her lap, she put on some makeup during the ride to the office. Miracle of miracles, she arrived at work only one minute late. She was feeling a good deal of personal triumph until she ran into Wes.

"Somebody sent you roses. Big, fat, red roses."

"Oh, really?" she asked nonchalantly, even though she was thrown into a full-on panic. Had Sawyer sent her flowers? She'd just been with him an hour ago. And to her job? He wouldn't do that. He wasn't that sort of guy. Or was he? He'd certainly seemed hell-bent on romance. He was being all seductive and impossible to resist, damn him.

She hurried back to her office. Sure enough, there on her desk sat a huge splay of long-stemmed roses in a tall glass vase, filling the room with a heady, sweet perfume. There had to be two dozen, and they were beautiful.

She closed her door behind her, so no one would see. There was a big part of her that wanted Sawyer to send her flowers. She wanted him to be that guy—hopelessly sweet and unafraid to make a grand gesture, even if it could get her in a heap of trouble. Her heart was beating a million miles a minute as she pulled the card out of the florist's envelope.

> For Kendall,
> With hopes that you'll accept my offer. I can't wait long.
> Fondly,
> James Locke

The blood in her veins went cold. She collapsed into her chair. A very powerful man with countless connections and endless means had just threatened her for the second time, in a way that was, quite frankly, chilling. The worst part of it was that she was falling for his son. And that might spell disaster.

Nine

Sawyer needed to look good for the Margaret Sharp interview—they were going to photograph him in the speakeasy, behind the bar. Unfortunately, he had to cut his shower short. His phone was going crazy.

"Noah?" he answered, putting the call on speakerphone so he could wrap a towel around his waist.

"Where have you been?" Noah's voice said he was out of breath. "I've been trying to get ahold of you."

"I was taking a shower."

"The hotel was vandalized."

Oh good God. No.

"I just got a call from Jerry. He was first on site this morning. I'm on my way over right now. You should do the same if you aren't already on your way."

Sawyer swiped at the fog on the mirror, shaking

his head. There was now no time to tidy up his facial hair. Kendall was going to kill him if he looked scraggly. Which might be fine. She'd been incredibly distant since they'd made love. "Yeah. Okay. I can be there in thirty."

"I guess it's bad."

"How bad?" Sawyer had visions of spray paint on the walls. Maybe a broken light fixture. The rooms that were the most important, and the most complete, were all locked up—the guest rooms, the apartments on the top floors, the grand ballroom and, of course, the speakeasy.

"I don't know, exactly."

Noah's voice left Sawyer with an uneasy feeling square in the middle of his chest. He was supposed to meet Kendall at nine. Margaret Sharp and her photographer were coming to the hotel at ten. And they couldn't afford yet another delay on the project. "I'm on my way."

He called Kendall from the car. He'd asked his driver to get him there as quickly as possible. "We might have a problem. Any chance we can reschedule the interview and photo session today?"

"What? Why? I've been working on this for two weeks, Sawyer. Margaret flew in from LA last night. I can't put her off. Nobody puts her off. Nobody."

Sawyer's phone beeped with a call from Noah. "Kendall, I'm sorry. Noah's on the other line. I have to take this. All I can tell you is there's been vandalism at the hotel and Noah said it's bad. I'm on my way there now."

"Oh no. I'm getting in a cab right now."

Sawyer didn't have time for fond farewells. He had to pick up the other line. "Hey. Sorry. On the line with Kendall."

"I almost don't want you to come, Sawyer. It's so much worse than bad. This is going to put us so far behind."

Sawyer wasn't sure which was worse—thinking about how bad it might be or actually seeing it. He only knew that he'd come too far to stop now. He wouldn't let his dad stop him, if that was the case. "We'll figure this out just like we've figured out everything else. I should be there in five minutes."

He hung up the phone and watched out the window at the city passing by. His whole history was tied to New York. He loved it more than anything, but there were times when it felt as though this city was going to be the death of him. Would it be better if he just turned his back on the Grand Legacy, sold it and moved as far from his father as possible? Buy a hotel in Fiji, languish under blue skies, ankle-deep in crystal-clear water anytime he wanted, trade in his tailored suit for a bathing suit, and live out his days with a drink in one hand, in peace? Maybe he could convince Kendall to join him. It was a nice idea. Probably too nice.

The car rolled up in front of the Grand Legacy and Sawyer climbed out, taking a deep breath, reminding himself to keep his temper in check. People were counting on him. It was his job to be the calm and measured one.

"Sawyer!" Kendall's voice came from behind him

and he turned to see her getting out of a cab. "I came as quickly as I could."

The sight of her was as welcome as the thoughts of Fiji and adopting a life that in no way resembled his current one. Leave it to him to entertain thoughts of third and fourth dates with a woman determined to keep her distance. "I haven't been in yet. I have no idea what we're walking into."

"No reason to panic yet. I postponed our session with Margaret, but I can't put her off forever."

It took every bit of self-control Sawyer had not to pull her into his arms or at least take her hand. Not knowing what was waiting inside, he craved her touch.

They made their way past the daytime security—that was going to have to be around the clock now. There'd be no more relying on alarm systems, high-tech gadgetry and security cameras at night. There would be actual people on site at all times.

He and Kendall stepped into the lobby, where Noah was waiting for them. The room was uncharacteristically quiet for a weekday. It felt a bit like walking into a graveyard. "Kendall, this is my brother, Noah."

"Nice to meet you," Noah said as he shook her hand. It was a strong indication of how upset his brother was—he hardly looked at Kendall. Noah did not pass up the chance to chat up a beautiful woman.

"You, too."

"Where are the crews?" Sawyer asked.

"I sent everyone except Jerry home. We need to keep this under our hats. Otherwise we have another fifty people who know what's going on. I made up an excuse about an inspection."

"Smart. I'm glad you're thinking straight about this." Sawyer clapped him on the back.

"I'm not thinking straight. And I don't think you will be either once you see this."

"Please. No more waiting. Let's just get this over with. Where are we headed?"

"The speakeasy."

Sawyer wasn't sure he heard anything at all as they took the back stairs up to the bar. Noah was talking nonstop about what would need to be fixed, but Sawyer had to see it for himself. As it turned out, a powerful chemical smell was the first indication something was wrong. It grew stronger as he climbed each stair. He was afraid to ask what it was.

Kendall was right behind him, not saying a word. Her presence was difficult for him to grapple with. He wanted her there. By now she was as integral a part of this project as anyone. But he also didn't want her pulled into his family drama. He didn't want to give her even more proof that very little behind the scenes with the Lockes was ever pretty.

Noah opened the wood back entry door, the one with the small circular window that mirrored the design of the window on the front of the hotel. It all happened in slow motion as Sawyer stepped inside and caught the first glimpse. Upholstery was slashed. Drywall had been torn down to the studs. The art deco metal screens between the booths had all been toppled, and were nothing more than gnarled pieces of scrap. The pendant light fixtures above the bar were smashed. Glass covered the carpet like uncut diamonds.

Kendall gasped. Sawyer couldn't manage a single sound. It was as if twenty hands were clasped around his throat and he was powerless to fight for words. He took another step and the carpet squished beneath his feet. "What the?"

"They poured something all over the carpet. A cleaning product, we think. I wouldn't walk around on it too much."

"Is it just this room? Please tell me they didn't get to the ceiling in the grand ballroom."

"It was all in here," Noah answered. "But you and I both know this is a disaster. The amount of custom work in this space could put us behind by months."

Right now, he wasn't thinking about how long it would take to catch up. He was too stuck on one detail. The destruction was limited to the speakeasy. This was more than an act of vandalism. It was a message. Sent directly by his father.

Sawyer felt something in the center of his back, then Kendall's voice, the only pleasant thing in this room. "It's okay. It's going to be okay. I'll get the interview rescheduled for later this afternoon so you can do whatever it is you need to work on this morning. We'll tell Margaret this room isn't ready to be photographed."

"What are you going to say? We specifically said we wanted this room featured."

"I'll tell them it was premature. The finishing touches are still being finalized. We'll focus on the grand ballroom. That's enough of a showpiece and no one has seen that ceiling look like that since the 1950s. It's still an exclusive. She'll still get what she wants."

"Do you think she'll be suspicious?"

She shrugged. "Honestly? I have no idea. We'll just have to do our best to make it all seem perfectly normal. I suggest you plan on answering every single one of her questions, no matter what."

"What does that mean?"

"I mean that if you are forthcoming about everything she asks, it will make Margaret feel like she came away with something special. The rooms aren't as important as the story. She wants to know that she has what no one else has."

Sawyer wasn't sure about this, at all, but he had to trust Kendall. He didn't have any other choice.

Kendall's phone rang. She caught a peek at the screen and her stomach sank. *Wes.* "I'm sorry, Sawyer. I have to take this."

"Hey, Wes. Good morning." Wes would make her life a living hell if she was confrontational, but being pleasant with him was painful. She ducked into the service hall outside the speakeasy.

"Why is Margaret Sharp's assistant calling me and complaining that you're leaving her in limbo? What in the hell is going on, Kendall?"

"I have no idea why they're calling you. I spoke to her directly this morning. Everything is under control." Except she had nothing under control, especially if Wes was going to get dragged into this.

"I thought you were at the Grand Legacy. Wasn't the interview supposed to be this morning?"

"I am at the Grand Legacy." She hesitated before she said another thing, still paranoid about James Locke's threats, especially after the flowers. Had the vandalism been prompted by her refusal to help him? It had been two days since she got the roses and she never responded, nor had she mentioned it to Sawyer. "We had to move the interview back a few hours. There was a chemical spill. I had to know the building was safe before she came in."

He grumbled. "This is a nightmare. I need to get Jillian up to speed. She needs to know that things are falling apart."

Kendall didn't grit her teeth often, but she was now. "Do not bother Jillian with this. The interview is going to happen, it's going to be amazing and Sawyer will do an incredible job. That's all that matters."

"You know, I can't help but notice how fond you are of Sawyer Locke."

"What's that supposed to mean?"

"I've seen the way you look at him when he comes into the office."

"What? Like he's my most important client and I want to make sure he has my undivided attention? How else do you suggest I look at him?"

"Calm down. I was just making an observation."

"Well, it's an inaccurate one and I need to go."

"Is that who sent you those flowers?"

Kendall's stomach churned. "I don't have time for this. I have an interview to set up for."

"Make it happen, please. I'm tired of putting out your fires."

Wes hung up on her, which only annoyed Kendall more. She really wished she could've hung up on him. But there was no time to think about that now. The chemical smell was making her sick to her stomach, although it seemed like everything was making her queasy these days. She went downstairs to the lobby outside the grand ballroom, and made a quick phone call to Margaret's hotel, first asking them to arrange an elegant lunch for Margaret and her photographer. Then, somehow, she talked Margaret into another post-ponement of the interview.

Sawyer emerged from the stairwell. She noticed for the first time that he was wearing exactly what she'd asked him to wear for the interview—gray suit, white shirt, dark tie. He looked good enough to eat, but she also saw the weariness in his eyes. The poor guy had been through the ringer with the hotel. However much she loved to look at him, she hated seeing him like this.

"Can you let me in?" She nodded at the grand ball-room doors. "I need to get us all set up in there."

"Yes. Of course." He pulled out his master key and unlocked the room, walking in with her and flipping on the lights. "I'm so sorry about today. I know this has made a lot more work for you."

"Part of the job, Sawyer. It's not a big deal." She had to mention what was weighing so heavily on her mind. "Plus, there's a good chance this is because of me."

"What do you mean?"

"Your dad. It's so obvious he's behind this, and I think it's because I refused to help him."

Sawyer placed his hand on her shoulder, leaving behind a warm tingle, followed by frustration. "No. Do not blame yourself. My father put you in an impossible position and you said no to his face, which isn't easy. Most people crumble in his presence."

"He sent me flowers. At work. Two days ago. Saying he wanted me to consider his offer."

Sawyer ran his hands through his hair. "Why didn't you tell me?"

"Because I saw how upset you got the day he waited on my street. And they were just flowers. I threw them in the dumpster behind my office and tried to forget about them."

He reined her in with his arms. "I'm so sorry you got pulled into this. I want you to know that I'll never forget your loyalty to me. You've really gone above and beyond."

Kendall stood there, in his arms, wanting this instant to be her reality—where Sawyer protected her, wanted her, and they could ignore her boss or his dad if they chose to. "I can't help but be loyal to you." It was true. She couldn't imagine being disloyal to him. Not now.

He patted her on the back and separated himself from her. "Part of the job, right?"

That was a dagger to the heart. She'd been loyal to no one but herself when she'd insisted the other morning that they stay away from each other. That couldn't have felt good to hear. It certainly hadn't been fun to say. "Yes, Sawyer. It's part of my job. But that doesn't mean I don't care."

"I know." He shook his head. "I'm sorry. Today is a nightmare."

"Hopefully it'll get better. I'd better set up for Margaret," she said.

Sawyer nodded, seeming preoccupied. "Yeah. I need to make some phone calls and see about replacing everything that was destroyed." He walked out of the room, leaving her all alone in the grand and elegant space.

She set up a table for the interview, making sure there was water and herbal tea, at Margaret's request. Kendall's stomach grumbled, and she fished a protein bar out of her purse, scarfing it down. Her mind wouldn't stop whirring, fixated on work as she fielded calls about interviews with Sawyer and answered emails on her phone.

Two hours later, her phone buzzed with a text announcing Margaret's arrival. Kendall rushed down the hall into the main lobby, where Margaret and her photographer were waiting. Margaret's glossy white-blond hair was cut in a chin-length bob. She wore black from head to toe. Kendall had only met Margaret once, but it did feel as though a queen had arrived—with more than four decades of top-level experience, she was as close to media royalty as you could get. She wrote for only the biggest publications, and they were all honored to have her contributions. Margaret had a real knack for digging deeply personal things out of people. It would be interesting to see what she could pull out of Sawyer.

"Ms. Sharp." Kendall held out her hand.

"Ms. Ross. I certainly hope we'll have no more delays today. I have a red-eye to catch this evening."

"Of course. We'll get started right away."

Kendall quickly got them situated in the grand ballroom after Sawyer gave a brief tour. Margaret pulled out a thick notebook and pen along with a digital recorder. The photographer was setting up lighting on the other side of the room. When the interview started, Kendall hung back, not wanting to intrude. This was Sawyer's moment to shine.

Thirty or so minutes in, it was going well. Margaret had started out asking about the history of the hotel and what it meant to Sawyer. It brought a smile to Kendall's face to hear the stories, especially those from his childhood.

"My brother and sister and I have always loved the hotel. When we were little, we rode the elevators, we played hide-and-seek in the halls. We were always trying to catch the hotel cat."

"Ah, yes. Mr. Wiggins. A fluffy Persian, right?" Margaret was known for meticulous research.

Sawyer smiled. "Yes. Precisely. Of course, Mr. Wiggins is long gone, but my brother and I love seeing everything else about the hotel come back to life. It's nostalgic and special to us both. Charlotte has been overseas during the final phase of renovations, but I'm hoping she'll be back for the grand reopening."

"But the hotel means the most to you. You're steering this ship."

Sawyer sat back in his chair, seeming prideful, which

he had every reason to be. "Yes. It definitely means the most to me."

"Tell me why your great-grandfather willed the hotel to you and not your father."

"I honestly don't know when he made the decision, but I think it was during what ended up being my final visit to the hotel with him. He was very frail, but he wanted to meet me at the hotel restaurant for lunch one Saturday. I was sixteen. He and I had always had a great relationship. He knew how much I loved the hotel. It was declining at that point, which made him sad. He was well aware that my dad wanted it torn down, or at least gutted. I told him that it could be great again if we just showed it some love."

"And then what happened?"

Sawyer shrugged. "We started talking about the Mets and finished our lunch. He passed away a little less than a year later and that's when I found out he'd left the hotel to me."

Margaret flipped a page of her steno pad, scrawling down notes. "I get the sense that although you and your father have a contentious relationship, that started before the Grand Legacy became yours. Your mother passed away when you were a boy."

Kendall held her breath, sensing that this might be the moment when Margaret got especially personal.

"Yes. I was eleven."

"That must've been hard, especially since your father was remarried quickly, wasn't he?"

Sawyer was trying to play it cool, but Kendall had learned to read his body language by now. He rubbed the back of his neck, which was never a good sign. It meant he was stressed. "It was quick. Yes."

Margaret flipped back through her notes. "Only five months after your mother passed away."

"I guess that sounds about right. Give or take."

"And your stepmother moved into the Locke family estate with her own four children. That must've been a big adjustment. Her oldest son, Todd, is a year older than you, isn't he? So you were no longer the oldest."

"It was hard. I won't deny that."

Sawyer's answers were becoming shorter and shorter, and the tone in his voice edged toward defensive. Less telling. Kendall needed to intervene, to protect Sawyer and the interview. "Margaret, is it okay if we take a quick break? I'd like a minute with Mr. Locke, if that's okay."

Margaret turned around, looking square at Kendall. "Five minutes, Ms. Ross. I was just hitting my stride."

"Five minutes. Tops." She rushed over to Sawyer while Margaret got up from her seat. He was downing the remainder of a bottle of water while she crouched down in front of him. "Everything okay? You seem tense."

"She's getting into some unpleasant topics. I don't like feeling like anyone is digging into my personal past."

"Of course she's digging. She wants to find everything she couldn't unearth in her research. She's connecting dots."

"Like I said, not a fan."

She set her hand on his leg and looked up at him.

"Okay. I get it. I can't force you to talk about some-thing you don't want to discuss, but let me just tell you one thing. It's okay to show people a chink in the armor. It's okay to share the painful stuff. I promise it will help the hotel if people know more about you. If you're more real."

He exhaled through his nose, looking into her eyes. "Okay."

"Do you trust me?"

"I do."

She patted his leg. "Okay, then. Talk to her. Answer her questions."

Margaret took her seat again. "Let's fast-forward a little bit. You went into the navy after college. You were injured and discharged."

Sawyer told the story he'd told Kendall the night at his apartment. Kendall couldn't stop picturing the scar on his shoulder. There was something so beautiful about it, a tiny glimpse of how human he really was.

"And what happened when you came back home? Was that a difficult readjustment?"

"It wasn't easy to step back into civilian life, but mostly because I had it in my head that I would be serv-ing for a while. Things changed quickly. And they were not the same when I got back."

"Can you elaborate on that?"

Sawyer cast his eyes over at Kendall. From twenty feet away, she could see how wounded he was. It made her want to hold on to him and tell him everything would be okay. She'd sensed there was a lot bubbling beneath the surface with him, and some of that had come out the other night, but it seemed clear right now that there was more. She couldn't breathe, waiting to hear what he was going to say.

Margaret rephrased her question. "Tell me what changed in your life while you were deployed overseas."

Sawyer drew in a deep breath through his nose. "I got engaged the night before I shipped out. She was a girl I'd met in college. Stephanie."

"You were in love?"

"I thought we were. I mean, I never saw myself getting married. Ever. My dad has been married so many times and it never sat right with me. I was determined I wasn't going to be like him in that respect."

"And why is that?"

"Because it felt like he never grieved the loss of my mother. He just moved on like it was nothing. Like she was nothing. Obviously my siblings and I don't feel like she didn't matter. She mattered a great deal to us."

Kendall's heart ached at Sawyer's admission. No wonder he'd been so wistful, and untalkative, when she'd pointed out the photograph on his bureau.

"Tell me what happened with your engagement," Margaret said.

"I'd asked my brother, Noah, to look after Stephanie while I was overseas. She lived in the city, not far from Noah. I guess it was just me being protective." He shifted in his seat. "Anyway, my dad invited them out to dinner at the family estate one weekend. I thought it was a great idea. Despite my relationship with my father, I wanted Stephanie folded into our family if possible.

Unfortunately, my dad had also invited my stepbrother, Todd, that night."

Kendall was filled with a deep sense of dread. She already knew it hadn't worked out with Stephanie.

"The older stepbrother from your father's second marriage. What happened?"

Sawyer shrugged. "According to Noah, Todd went after her."

"Went after her?"

"Romantically. Noah said he'd never seen anything like it. He and Todd got into a big argument that night. Noah always has my back. Always. He took Stephanie home and then didn't hear anything about it, so he figured that he'd gotten through to Todd. That he'd convinced him that it was not okay for him to do that."

"Then what?"

"Noah ran into her three months later and she was wearing a different engagement ring. She'd taken off the one I'd given her and had gotten engaged to Todd instead."

Kendall's hand flew to her mouth. Her heart was going to pound its way out of her chest. No wonder he'd been so incredibly upset about the fake engagement ring. No wonder he'd spouted off at her about how it represented love and commitment. An engagement ring meant a lot to Sawyer, even more than it meant to the average person.

"Why didn't Stephanie tell you?" Margaret asked.

"I guess she didn't want to hurt me, but she ended up hurting me anyway. She'd stopped writing as many letters, and they'd had a very different tone to them, so I suspected something was happening, but I didn't know for sure, and then I got hurt. I got home after my injury and I found out exactly how much my life had fallen apart."

"Your own stepbrother."

"Yes. It was a pretty deep betrayal, by two people I trusted. Todd and I became close when we were teenagers. At least I thought we were. And of course, nobody wants to get dumped for someone else."

Kendall shook her head, aghast that anyone could do that, especially to a man as sweet and generous as Sawyer. And, of course, if his father had facilitated all of this, it was twice the betrayal.

"Those two actually ended up getting married," Sawyer continued. "My dad invited them to Christmas that year, even though Todd's mom wasn't around anymore because she'd passed away. Even though he knew I was going to be there, too. I had to skip Christmas with my family because I couldn't put myself through it."

"Your dad invited them for Christmas?"

Sawyer nodded. "Yes. He has a real talent for going for the jugular."

The hair on the back of Kendall's neck stood up. He'd done it. He'd told Margaret Sharp the sort of story that she loved to print. And now Kendall had a good guess as to why Sawyer was so detached, never getting involved, never calling women after one night. He wasn't being a playboy because he could. He was that way because he was protecting himself. He'd had his heart broken.

That realization left her with a truth of her own—the only thing she could think about right now was kissing away his pain.

Ten

Sawyer hadn't dared to dredge up those unhappy memories in a long time, but today he'd divulged painful things, many about his father. His dad had earned whatever Margaret Sharp was going to print. His father could hurt him, but Sawyer could hurt him right back.

Kendall, who had just bid Margaret and the photographer goodbye, was striding back into the grand ballroom, ever unflappable, and always—always—beautiful. She smiled and placed her hand on his shoulder. "Are you okay?" She looked up at him with wide eyes, full of concern.

"I'm better now that the interview is over and it's just us again." He had to be honest. He raked his fingers through his hair, fighting back the urges that were welling up inside him. Today had been utter hell. He wanted to feel good. He wanted an escape from his world, if only for a few minutes. And the respite he wanted more than anything was right in front of him. If ever a woman could make him lose all sense of time and space, it was Kendall.

"I know it's been a hard day. It couldn't have been easy to talk about those things."

"It wasn't easy, but I trust everything you said about it being the right thing to do."

She folded her hands in front of her, seeming deep in thought. "After hearing everything you said, I understand why you were so upset about the ring. I feel like such a fool for what I did."

He shook his head. "No. Don't. You did what you had to do for you. I respect that. I need to shed that particular sensitive spot, anyway."

"I know you want to be the tough guy, but taking off your engagement ring and putting on someone else's? That's brutal. Nobody could blame you for being sensitive about it."

"Doesn't mean I don't need to learn to let it go."

"You're amazing. You're so strong. I don't know if I could be so strong."

He laughed quietly, wanting so badly to take her hand, tug her closer. "I'm strong? You're the strongest, most determined person I have ever met."

She playfully socked him on the arm. "I am not."

"I'm not kidding. And all it makes me want to do right now is kiss you." He wrapped his arms around her waist.

Kendall's breath hitched. "Sawyer…"

He knew what she was about to launch into. "I know we said we wouldn't do this. I know it's wrong, but I want you. Every time I'm around you, it's this test that I can hardly bear."

Kendall glanced around the otherwise empty room then returned her sights to him. They were alone. He hadn't been that dumb. "I want you too, Sawyer. I do. I feel so bad about everything that happened today…"

He clutched her neck and brought her lips to his, if only to silence the pity. He didn't need her to feel sorry for him. He needed her to want him. Her kiss was instantly giving and insistent, her lips parting and welcoming his tongue. She was as hungry for him as he was for her. She pushed up onto her tiptoes, pressing her torso against his. Her enthusiasm made his hips and thighs pull taut. She wasn't stepping on the brake, she was stomping on the gas. He tugged her closer. As amazing as the kiss was, as much as he'd been thinking about it nonstop, he needed more of her and less of their clothes. "Can we go somewhere?" he asked.

"I want to, but it's a huge risk. Someone could see us." Kendall was breathless, her lips plump and red. The delicate skin around her mouth was pale pink from his scruff. He loved seeing evidence of just how ridiculously hot they were for each other.

"Nobody's here. The foremen went home. Noah went back to the office. Come on." He took her hand and led her out of the grand ballroom and across the waiting area to the fire stairs.

"We just went into the speakeasy. It's a disaster in there."

"Not where we're going."

Kendall came to a dead stop. "Oh, wait. They photographed guest rooms for the website yesterday, didn't they?"

He tugged on her arm. "Yes. Now, come on."

They got to the tenth floor, slightly out of breath. "Couldn't we have stopped three floors ago? I know they took pictures of a room on seven."

"You deserve better than that." He led her out into the hall and they hurried down the corridor. Sawyer's spine was like a metal spring pulled to its limit. The anticipation of exploring Kendall's sumptuous curves, sinking his fingers into her skin, was almost too much to take.

He fiddled with his keys, but it was as if his fingers had forgotten how to work. The electronic keycard system wasn't fully functioning yet, so he had to go the old-fashioned route and use a housekeeper's key. His head was pressed against the door while Kendall stood right next to him, softly running her fingers into the hair at his nape, her sweet honey scent hitting his nose and making it impossible to concentrate. Finally, he got the key jammed into the lock and the door open.

"Ladies first." Sawyer hung back for a second, if only to collect himself and gather the sexy thoughts going through his head right now. The things he wanted to do to Kendall…with Kendall. Could he play hooky for the rest of the day?

She stopped in the center of the room and looked back at him over her shoulder, her eyes piercing any sense of self-control he'd been able to muster. "This room is absolutely stunning. Everything is perfect."

You're perfect. He drew in one more look of her from head to toe.

"I love the tones of gray and silver and white, with the black accents. It's so elegant. Everything shimmers. The guests are going to be blown away by how gorgeous it is."

He had to touch her. "This room has nothing on you."

She turned to him, face flush with pink. "I practically handed you that line on a platter."

"I would've found a way to say it. But yes, you made it sound a lot smoother."

She rested her forearms on his shoulders as his hands went to her waist, caressing her full hips. She gazed up at him, a soft smile on her lips. The rosy flush on her cheeks, and the sparkle in her sapphire eyes, sucked the breath out of him. Was she glowing? "You were amazing today. I want you to know that," she said softly, punctuating it with a maddening lick of her lower lip.

He was not a man swayed by flattery, but the sweetness in her voice said just how deeply and sincerely she meant it. Admiration from Kendall was worth so much more than it was from anyone else. "Thank you. Thank you for being here. Thank you for supporting me. I don't know what I would be doing right now if we hadn't hired you."

She shook her head. "No work talk. If we talk about work, I'll just start to feel guilty that we're here in this room."

"No guilt. As far as I'm concerned, the rest of the world can go away. It's just you and me right now."

"And that beautiful bed." She trailed her fingers along his spine, driving him crazy.

He tugged her into an embrace and kissed her, their lips picking up right where they'd left off downstairs, a passionate impatience he'd never experienced with any other woman.

She arched into him, again up on her tiptoes, hands in his hair, her unforgettable lips making a mess of his mind. It was impossible to think and Sawyer had done more than enough thinking for one day.

"We have to get you out of this dress," he muttered against her lips.

Kendall turned her back to him, gathering her glossy hair and pulling it to the side. She again looked at him with that look…her eyes full of mischief and play. That was the look she'd given him at the wedding. That was the look that had first made him want her. He wrestled off his suit coat then turned his attention to her zipper, drawing it down. Every inch of her skin revealed was a gift, especially as he passed the strap of her black bra and sank lower to black lace-and-satin panties. He stood right behind her, pressing his body against hers, his fierce erection nestled between them. He was at war with himself, wanting his clothes off, absolutely wanting her clothes gone, while wanting to savor every moment, every bit of this feast for the senses. After last time, he'd thought this wasn't going to happen again.

He nudged her dress from her shoulders and it fell forward, slumping to the floor. He wrapped his arms around her naked waist, pulling her back against him, his hands cupping her incredible breasts, the lace-covered satin softly caressing his palms. He skimmed his lips over the velvety skin of her neck, and she dropped her head to the side, moaning softly. He brought his hands back to unhook her bra clasp, still kissing her neck as she shook the garment from her body. Her skin was too supple and smelled too good to stop kissing her.

He turned her around, cupping her breasts with his hands, her skin warm beneath his touch. He lowered his head to lick and suck her dark pink nipples. The skin tightened. He loved seeing her body react to his touch.

Her frantic fingers went to work on his shirt while he kept his attention focused on her luscious breasts. He could hold them and admire them for hours, but he had to let go for an instant to unbutton his cuffs and strip off his shirt. He reached for Kendall, but she surprised him, dropping to her knees and pressing the heel of her hand against his erection, making him impossibly hard. So much so that he nearly passed out from the rush of blood and heat. He sucked in a deep breath, steeling himself for more.

Metal clattered as she unbuckled his belt, then unbuttoned and unzipped his trousers. He quickly toed off his shoes and pulled off his socks. He shucked the pants then stood before her again, letting her take charge. Her fingers slipped below the waistband of his boxer briefs and she slowly tugged them down past his hips. As if she needed to seduce him right now…just being with her left him ready to rocket into space. She wrapped her fingers around his length and stroked. Their gazes connected, her grip firm, her eyes bright and intense.

She licked her lips and everything froze for a moment as he realized what came next.

She took him into her mouth, unbelievably warm and welcoming. Nothing had ever felt better than that—nothing had ever been so sweet and hot. She took her time, intent on his pleasure, and he had to watch, with the late afternoon light filtering into the room through the gauzy sheers. He dug his fingers into her silky hair, caressing gently. Her lips on him was one of the sexiest images he'd ever seen, and as gratifying as it was, the truth was that he had to have her. All of her.

He reached down and tugged on her arms, bringing her back to standing. He walked her back to the bed and she reclined onto the pure white duvet, sinking down into the puffiness. All he could think about was getting lost in her.

Kendall arched her back, the silky sheets skimming her skin. The only thing better was the view of Sawyer as he towered over her, completely naked. The wry smile on his face was only improved by the dark shadow of scruff along his jaw, the way he cocked an eyebrow at her. Every inch of him was perfect—sculpted shoulders, firm chest with just the right amount of dark hair, trailing down between his well-defined abs. She was dying to have him inside her, and judging by just how hard he'd been in her hand and mouth, he felt the same way. "Come here," she said, curling her finger.

"I was only admiring the view," he countered, reaching down and shimmying her panties past her hips.

She scooted back on the bed and he settled next to

her, kissing her softly, while his hands cupped her bottom, fingers digging into her flesh, and he pulled her closer. "I want you, Sawyer," she said, finding a new weight in the words now. She'd read him all wrong. Did that mean there could be something real between them? Or was there too much on the line? His hotel, her job, the project.

Sawyer rolled her to her back, kissing her lips, then her jaw and her neck again. He positioned himself between her legs and drove inside, filling her perfectly. They rocked together, Kendall wrapping her legs around him and holding him close. She wanted to cherish every moment of this. They shouldn't have put themselves in this situation, not with the professional conflicts, but there was something wonderful about having this secret between them. It was theirs. Sawyer was right. The rest of the world *could* go away. It should go away.

She closed her eyes and focused on the here and now—the sensations of tension building inside her, the sound of his breaths as they grew shorter, the pressure of his body weight against hers, keeping her safe, making her feel adored and cherished. It was a beautiful day when the sun of Sawyer Locke chose to shine down on you.

Her peak was approaching quickly. Sawyer was simply too adept at finding a woman's sweet spots. She was so thankful for it. The pleasure rolled through her like a pebble tumbling down a slope, faltering and starting, but unable to stop. Sawyer soon followed, taking several forceful thrusts and calling out. He settled his face in her neck, catching his breath, and Kendall tried to catch her heart, which felt like it might splinter into hundreds of pieces. She couldn't escape the feeling that what was between them was more than lust or attraction. It felt much more basic and essential, like air and water.

They remained entwined on the bed for several moments, Kendall doing everything she could to switch her brain back into work mode. The countless barriers, the enormous gray area between them, might make her cry. How was Sawyer going to get the hotel back on schedule? Maybe they could move the grand opening to February. Valentine's Day. That could be sweet and fun.

But she couldn't get past the idea that the longer things dragged out, the more opportunities James Locke would have to interfere. They had to give him fewer chances to do his damage. And they had to catch him off guard.

"I have a crazy idea," Kendall said.

"With most people, I'd say no before you even got it out of your mouth."

"You're in a tough spot with the vandalism and getting back on schedule."

"You're ruining the mood, just so you know."

"I'm serious, Sawyer. You and Noah are going to have to figure out what exactly it is that you're doing. The entire launch of the hotel depends on the grand reopening."

"Yeah. I was thinking about that. What if we move it to Valentine's Day? We'd have another six weeks, which should be enough to get us to where we need to be. It'll still be tight, but I think we can do it."

"Yeah. I thought about that, too, but I'm not sure it's

the best idea." Kendall gnawed on her lower lip. Sawyer didn't seem like the type to blow his top, but what she was about to suggest might send his stress level through the roof. "I was actually thinking of moving in the other direction."

For a moment, he just stared at her. Not in shock. Not in surprise. Just stared. Unflinching. Unblinking. "As in earlier? That's your idea?"

She scrunched up her face and nodded. "I told you it was crazy. But just hear me out. December fifth. The day Prohibition was repealed."

"The fifth. Of December. This year. You are aware it's almost the end of October."

"Yes. Just think about it. It's perfect. That day was celebrated at the hotel every year. It was bigger than New Year's Eve. Much bigger. You know why?"

He shook his head. "No clue."

"Because nobody else is throwing a big party on December fifth. Nobody." Kendall braced for Sawyer's reaction, but to her great delight, she could see the gears starting to turn in Sawyer's brain. "The whole world has a party on New Year's Eve. You were already going to have to compete with the ball drop in Times Square and everything else going on all over the city. If you have it on December fifth, there's no competition. And it ties into the hotel's history, which makes my job a lot easier."

"You realize this is literally the last thing my dad will be expecting."

She smiled and nodded. "Exactly. He'll be thinking this will knock you off track and off schedule. So you do the opposite. You open three weeks earlier than expected."

Sawyer slumped back in bed. "But how do we do that? Three weeks. Do you have any idea how long it took us to have just the metal screens made?"

"The fabricator already has the designs, right? That must've been a big part of the timeline before."

"It was."

"So call and beg them to drop everything and remake them."

"I don't beg, Kendall. It's not my style."

"Fine. Then throw around some money and the Locke name. That has to be good for something."

Sawyer laughed. "The money, yes. The Locke name, I'm not so sure anymore."

Eleven

A meeting would likely accomplish nothing, but Sawyer and Noah had agreed that they had to put their dad on notice. Sawyer had volunteered. One thing wouldn't stop eating at him—the threat to Kendall. After they'd made love at the Grand Legacy, he realized that she had become the good in his day, the sunshine after the rain, the blossom blooming in the snow. He'd waited a long time to have that in his life, and he had to protect her at all costs because of it.

He had his driver take him out to the family estate on Long Island—eleven acres on the water, with spectacular views of Mecox Bay and all the trappings of the Locke family fortune: tennis courts, two pools, a dozen bedrooms and a kitchen as large as a bowling alley. Sawyer didn't bother to call ahead. It was one of the many games he and his dad played. James always made Sawyer talk his way past the layers of security. Going home was like storming the castle. Sawyer had done it many times.

Tom, the guard manning the iconic stone and iron gate onto the Locke property, had been on staff since Sawyer was a young boy. He walked out to the car, shaking his head, smiling. "I shouldn't let you in, Sawyer. But not that long ago, it was my job to protect you, so I'm not about to keep you out."

"I appreciate that, Tom." Even Sawyer's dad didn't have an answer for Tom's reasoning.

The car crept ahead, over the crushed stone of the drive edged by manicured lawn and sculpted hedges, all the way up to the sprawling white house with the black slate roof, rising up out of a stand of autumn-colored trees. When he was young, this house was home and he loved it. It wasn't until later that Sawyer realized it didn't mean much without the love of his mother keeping them all together.

A member of the security detail was out front when the car reached the house. After some back and forth, Sawyer was allowed inside, where he was made to wait in the parlor outside his father's home office for a good fifteen to twenty minutes. His dad was busy, but he wasn't *that* busy. It was all for show.

"Your father will see you now," said his dad's secretary.

"Thanks." Sawyer marched in and sat down opposite his father's tank of a desk. You'd think he was the president in the oval office, judging by the furniture in the room.

"How nice of you to drop by." His dad scrawled on a pad of paper, not bothering to look up at Sawyer. "It might be nice if you called first. Catherine would love to see you. She is your stepmother after all."

"I wouldn't call her my stepmother. She's your wife. I was twenty-nine when you got married."

"Do you know what your problem is, Sawyer?"

"No. But I'm sure you're going to tell me."

"You're wound too tight. You always have been." He sat back in his chair. "You need to get married and have a few kids. Enjoy life. You'll end up with high blood pressure if you don't watch it."

Sawyer could've gone for the jugular, reminded his dad of the things he did to contribute to his stress levels, but that wasn't what he'd come for today. "If anyone knows the health benefits of marriage, you do."

"I've been lucky enough to find four women who wanted to be my wife. There's no shame in that. I've loved them all."

Not equally, Sawyer thought. That had been the saddest revelation after his mother passed away. Sawyer, Noah and Charlotte were still grieving the loss of their mother when their father married his second wife, Abigail. She moved into their house with her four kids, and even though there was plenty of room for everyone, Sawyer couldn't help but feel put out and left out. When he'd dared to bring this up to his dad, to actually share his feelings, his dad accused him of trying to kill his happiness. He then delivered the line that would forever remain in Sawyer's mind: *I never loved your mother like I love Abigail. She's the real love of my life.*

For a boy mourning his mother, it had felt as though his father had sent every happy memory of his mother up in flames. Everything was tarnished from then on. Well, at least until Abigail also died, and the third wife came along. His dad delivered the same line about her and that was when Sawyer deduced it wasn't about who his father was married to. His dad was in love with the idea of romance, and he went through women accordingly. It was such a bizarre contrast to his father's otherwise ruthless ways, but Sawyer had long ago stopped trying to figure out his dad.

"I'm here to broker a truce over the Grand Legacy. The vandalism went too far."

"I read about it in the paper. Terrible setback."

"Don't worry. We'll still reopen. Just not when we'd originally planned to." He kept his voice even, but the inner sense of triumph he had about executing Kendall's new plan was immense.

"Oh, it must not have been that bad then."

"You're going to sit here and act as though you don't know."

"I'm not the only one who wants the history of the hotel to be left in the past. Your marketing plan made it so much worse. Calling it the most notorious hotel in the city? It's like you want to send our family reputation straight into the gutter."

Sawyer kneaded his forehead. "You spend too much time worrying about appearances. The history of the hotel is fascinating to people. Nobody thinks badly of our family for things that aren't even illegal anymore."

"Believe me, plenty of things went on in that hotel that are still very illegal. Your great-grandfather had some very shady partners at the beginning. People who feel they never got their fair share."

This caught Sawyer's attention. His father was always very vague when he spoke about the shadier side of the hotel's past. "Why didn't you tell me this before? There's no paperwork that even makes mention of a partnership."

"We aren't talking about people who like to leave a paper trail, Sawyer. Honestly, I shouldn't even be talking to you about this. The less you know, the better. I don't know why you won't believe me when I say that."

"Dad. I have millions of dollars on the line. I'm not a kid, and I can't make business decisions based on anything but facts. So if there are actual details you care to share with me, please do."

"Like I said, the less you know, the better."

Sawyer grumbled under his breath. "We need to talk about Ms. Ross. I want you to stay away from her. I don't want you to communicate with her in any way, especially not by sending flowers." The steadiness in his voice had failed. The idea of Kendall being in his father's sights was more upsetting than he cared to admit.

"I guess I have my answer then, since she decided to tell you. You must have done something quite extraordinary to warrant that kind of loyalty."

"Kendall has a conscience and she's committed to

her job." The room grew eerily quiet. Sawyer shifted in the antique chair he was sitting in, which creaked.

"You seem pretty worked up about this woman. Is there something you aren't telling me? A little romance I don't know about?"

Sawyer had done his best to keep his feelings concealed. Perhaps he wasn't as good at being poker-faced as he thought. "I'm not going to discuss Kendall."

His father cocked an eyebrow. "So there is a romance. There's hope for you, yet."

"Please don't speak to me like that. I don't need your help or your blessing or anything. Just please leave Kendall alone. She has nothing to do with your obsession with the hotel. I'm merely asking you to leave her alone."

"It's not an obsession. I'm trying to keep our family in one piece. The Locke name is everything. The money and the business mean nothing without it. Some day, you'll have children of your own and you'll understand how important it is. If you and your brother aren't careful, you're going to hand them something damaged."

The fire smoldering in Sawyer's belly began to roar. His father was far guiltier of damaging the family name, and the actual family for that matter. As far as Sawyer was concerned, the business of having children and handing down the Locke name would not be carried out by him. There was too much poison running through this family line. "In case you haven't noticed, I'm not trying to follow in your footsteps."

"Passing on the Locke name is of paramount importance, Sawyer."

"This happens every time we talk about the Grand Legacy. You start going on about the family name. I'm reopening the hotel. I'm seeing Great-Grandpa's dream to fruition. That's my way of honoring the family name. It will be just as amazing as it once was. You'll see that your paranoia about it has been for nothing."

"If your mother was still alive, she'd agree with me."

Sawyer's eyes narrowed. "What does my mother have to do with it?"

His father cleared his throat and shifted in his seat. "You don't know everything there is to know about your mother and her family. She wasn't the perfect woman you thought she was."

Sawyer had had enough. He stood and headed for the door. "I'm leaving now. I'm not going to listen to you talk about her that way. You didn't even love her. You told me as much."

"We were young. We thought we were in love. We weren't."

Every word out of his father's mouth was designed to cut, but Sawyer wouldn't let him get away with it. Not today. "Goodbye, Dad." He opened the door, when his dad's voice came right behind him.

"If you want to find out who vandalized the Grand Legacy, you need to look somewhere outside the confines of this office."

Sawyer closed his eyes. More manipulation. That was all that was. "All signs point to you, but nice job deflecting."

* * *

Kendall had finally broken down and made a doctor's appointment. Sure, work was crazy, but her fatigue wasn't normal. Now that Sawyer had agreed to the new, tighter timeline, Kendall had to be on her A game. Getting sick would ruin everything.

Things at the office were beyond busy, leaving Kendall with no choice but to forgo lunch so she could take that hour, get to her doctor's appointment and figure out once and for all if she was getting the flu.

"Ms. Ross," the nurse called.

Kendall set down the magazine she'd been flipping through, and followed. The nurse took her blood pressure and recorded her weight, then showed her to an exam room.

"The doctor will be in shortly."

Kendall sat on the exam table, kicking her legs. It was nice to be in a room that was completely quiet. No boss yelling from the other room. No sound of fire trucks whizzing by, like at home. If only she could turn off these horrific fluorescent lights, lie down and get in a nap.

A knock came at the door. "Hello, Kendall," Dr. Adams said. She shook her hand and took a seat on the physician's rolling stool. She plucked a pair of red reading glasses from her pocket and put them on, then smoothed back her shoulder-length gray hair. "What can I do for you today?"

"I haven't been feeling well. I'm really run-down, my stomach is unsettled and I'm ridiculously tired. All I want to do is sleep."

Dr. Adams wheeled her way closer. "Any congestion? Headaches?"

Kendall shook her head. "I've been a little stuffy, but not like I was last time with the sinus infection."

"Fever? Body aches?"

"Nope."

The doctor stood and reached for the otoscope on the wall. "Alright then. Let's take a look." She pulled at Kendall's earlobes and after a few seconds, replaced the instrument. "Any chance you could be pregnant?"

"I thought you were checking my ears."

Dr. Adams laughed. "I was. But you have an awful lot of symptoms that could be attributed to a pregnancy. No fever. Tired and run-down."

"I'm not pregnant." Of course she wasn't. Absolutely not. "I'm on the pill. It's in my chart."

Dr. Adams nodded, standing up. "Let's do a quick test to rule it out, though. Let me feel your glands. I apologize if my hands are cold." She placed her fingers on Kendall's neck.

"Is a pregnancy test really necessary? I don't see any way I could be pregnant." Her mind began to start and stop. Her last period had been unusually light, but she hadn't thought anything of it. She'd just been thankful. *Could I be? No. No way.*

"It's not a big deal. Just a quick trip to the bathroom."

Dr. Adams wrote down a few things, but Kendall wasn't paying much attention. The thing was, if she was indeed pregnant, which was the most ridiculous idea ever, there was only one person who could be the father. She'd only been with one man in the last year. Sawyer.

"You seem perfectly healthy to me. You might just be fighting something off, but let's rule out a pregnancy. We should go ahead and get you a flu shot while you're here, as well."

Kendall clutched Dr. Adams's arm. "How could I get pregnant on the pill? How does that happen?"

Dr. Adams's glasses slid to the end of her nose as she peered at Kendall. "Have you been sexually active?"

A flush crossed Kendall's cheeks like she was a teenager. "Well, yeah. But isn't that the whole point of the pill?"

"It is, but it's not foolproof. And you were on antibiotics two months ago for a sinus infection. Those reduce efficacy. It should've said on the pill bottle to use backup contraception."

"It didn't. I definitely know it didn't say that. Should I complain to the pharmacy?"

"Kendall. This isn't something you can argue your way out of. Either you are or you aren't. So let's find out, shall we?"

Kendall shrank back, realizing just how ridiculous she was being. "Yes. Right. Of course." It was probably nothing. Still, she couldn't feel her hands or her toes right now. Everything was a little numb.

The nurse came in and handed Kendall a plastic cup. "Out in the hall, the bathroom is the second room on the left. Follow the instructions and leave the specimen on the shelf. You can get dressed after that. It'll just take a few minutes for the results."

Kendall did as she was told, focusing on following the directions posted on the bathroom wall to the letter of the law. When she was done, she went back to the exam room and sat in the chair and waited. *Why is it taking so long? Why is it so cold in here?* She checked her phone. She'd been gone from the office for nearly an hour. Jillian would not be happy. Kendall had been gone for the entire day yesterday.

Another knock came at the door. Kendall turned, expecting to see the nurse again, but it was the doctor. *Oh no.*

"Well, it looks as though you're going to need to stop taking your birth control pills. The test was positive. You're pregnant."

Kendall had no clue how one was expected to react to this news when it was the last thing you were expecting. "Thank you."

"Thank you?"

She stood and shook her head. *What is wrong with me? Oh, wait. I know. I'm pregnant. With Sawyer Locke's baby. That's what's wrong with me.* "I'm sorry. Just a little shell-shocked, I guess." *I guess? I'm definitely shell-shocked. I'm beyond shocked. I'm flabbergasted.*

"Perfectly understandable. I'd call your gynecologist when you have a chance so you can make your first appointment. Until then, make sure you're taking a multivitamin, get your rest, drink plenty of fluids."

Kendall stood there, information flowing from the doctor's mouth into her ears, but it was so slow to sink in…it was like syrup on a waffle. Sitting there one minute, gone the next. "Okay."

"As long as you take care of yourself, you'll be taking care of the baby."

Baby. Coming to terms with the word *pregnant* was one thing, but the word *baby* was a leap she was not prepared to take. *A baby. I'm going to have a baby? I'm going to have a baby.* "Thank you" was again all she could mutter as she wandered out of the exam room, down the hall, paid her co-pay just like she had two months ago when she'd had the sinus infection. When she got out to the street, she didn't know what to do, where to go. Technically, she belonged at work. It was after one and now she'd been away for over an hour.

She hopped in a cab, feeling as alone as she'd felt in a long time. Moments like this were the ones when she most missed her mom. They hadn't always agreed, but her mom was an eager confidante. Sometimes a bit too quick with advice, but Kendall had always listened. Her mom had gone through a lot, more than any person should ever have to—single mom; abandoned by the guy who got her pregnant; endless string of bad, commitment-phobic boyfriends; never found her purpose. Well, other than Kendall. Perhaps raising a daughter had been her purpose. Thinking that way only made Kendall feel worse. She had so much to live up to. If her mom's only purpose had been her, what did she have to show for it? An uncertain promotion and an unplanned pregnancy with a man she hardly knew, whose own father had threatened her.

Wrong turn or not, she had to tell Sawyer right away. She couldn't work with him and keep this sort of secret from him. He'd told her from the beginning that he needed to be able to trust her.

She pulled out her cell phone to make the call before she got back to the office.

He picked up after the third ring. "Kendall. Tell me something good. Anything."

"What? What are you talking about?"

"I'm in the car on my way back into the city. I just had a showdown with my dad. It was ridiculous."

Kendall closed her eyes and shook her head. "Was that a good idea?"

"Probably not, but I can't take all of this lying down."

Great. Maybe his bad mood can't get any worse. "Are you free tonight? I need to see you."

"Oh, really?" His voice dipped an octave.

"Not that, Sawyer. I need to talk to you. In person. Can I come to your office?"

"You first have to tell me you aren't going to give me any bad news about the hotel. I can't handle it right now."

"Nothing about the hotel. I promise. Your office?"

"You haven't told me what we're talking about."

"I need to say this in person, isn't that enough?"

"What about the Club? On Lexington? I could use a good steak."

"A restaurant? Don't you think that's a bad idea?"

"Kendall. If you aren't going to tell me what we're talking about, I can't pick a place. I want a steak for dinner. Just indulge me, okay?"

"You aren't worried about tempting fate?" Talk about tempting fate—she never should've said yes when

Sawyer asked her to dance at the wedding. Then she wouldn't be in this situation at all.

"It'll be fine."

The cab pulled up in front of her office. She had to get back to work or Jillian would have her hide. "Fine. The Club. Eight?"

"Perfect. I'll make reservations."

Twelve

Kendall got out of the cab in front of the restaurant Sawyer had asked her to meet him at for dinner. She'd told him it wasn't a good idea, that he needed to stop acting as though they could continue to tempt fate like this. His attitude about it? He just wanted a steak.

She stepped inside the restaurant simply known as the Club, which she'd never been to but had heard so much about. It was classic romance—dark, secluded booths, candles flickering on white tablecloths, words spoken in hushed tones over champagne and martinis.

"I'm meeting Mr. Locke," she said to the hostess.

"Of course, Ms. Ross. Daniel here will take your wrap." Before Kendall knew what was happening, a mysterious man was behind her, waiting for her to take off her coat. "This way."

Sawyer was off in the corner, looking far more handsome than was fair. Even from a distance, she could see that his usual five o'clock shadow was hours old, darkening his face, accentuating the chiseled lines. He stood as soon as he caught sight of her, and he smiled. It was a genuine smile, the kind you only get from a man after you've slept with him, the kind of smile that makes your knees turn to rubber. If things were different between them, that smile would've warmed her from head to toe. It would've been a sign that everything in her world was right. Instead, it only reminded her of what she couldn't count on, of the ways in which her life was veering off course right now. A baby had never been part of her plan.

"You look stunning," he said, kissing her on the cheek.

"Thank you. But is that something you would typically say to a work associate? Because something tells me it isn't." She slid into the booth and placed her purse between them.

"It absolutely isn't. But I've never worked with anyone as beautiful as you, nor have I ever worked with anyone I've been in bed with, so this is new territory for me. I think we should be able to say nice things to each other when it's just the two of us."

She shifted in her seat, feeling an unbearable urge to rid herself of her burdensome secret. "Sure. That's fine. You look very nice yourself."

"Thank you." He took a sip of his drink. "The waiter should be here any minute to take your drink order. They make a spectacular Manhattan."

Sure enough, a waiter arrived at their table. "Ma'am, can I get you anything from the bar?"

"Cranberry juice, please."

"Certainly. And are we ready to order or do we need a few minutes?"

"The New York strip is fantastic," Sawyer said to Kendall. "That's what I'll have. Medium-rare, please."

"And for the lady?" the waiter asked.

Kendall didn't have the mental capacity to read a menu right now. "I'll have the same. Medium. Please."

"Right away."

"Not drinking tonight?" Sawyer asked.

"No. I wasn't really feeling it." *And everyone knows you shouldn't drink when you're pregnant.*

"Maybe you'll change your mind later. I know I really needed it. I've needed one all afternoon, to be honest."

"Let me guess. The talk with your dad?"

He nodded. "I had to talk to him after he pulled that stunt with you, especially if the vandalism was his way of responding. And I'm sorry, but the flowers were just creepy. I couldn't live with myself if I didn't tell him to stay away from you, and it wouldn't have the same effect if I didn't do it in person."

"Sawyer. I really hope you didn't provoke your dad because of me. That's a terrible idea. The whole thing really wasn't a big deal. I'm perfectly capable of taking care of myself."

"But he threatened you. It's one thing to mess with the hotel, but when it comes to people, especially you, that's unacceptable."

Kendall settled her hands in her lap, her circumstances pressing down on her like an unbearable weight. How had everything spiraled out of control like this? Just a few short months ago, she had everything in hand. Then she went to that wedding and Sawyer Locke walked into her life. Now she was pregnant by him, the son of a man who had stalked her on the streets of New York and threatened her livelihood. This was the sort of situation her mother would unwittingly get herself into, and Kendall had had to stand by and watch many times as her mother struggled to find a way out of it. It never ended well.

A baby. She was going to have a baby. How was she going to make this work? In her tiny apartment in a not-safe neighborhood, as James Locke had been so generous to point out, with far more than a full-time job. She had a career that demanded, at minimum, sixty hours of her time each week. She would need childcare, a nursery and a million other things she couldn't even think about right now. Forget sleep. She wasn't going to see any of that for a long time.

Sawyer placed his hand on her shoulder, his warmth pouring into her, warmth that she feared would never last. "Everything okay?"

"This has gone far beyond my normal involvement with a client, Sawyer. I mean, ridiculously beyond. It's a lot to deal with." *Just tell him. Just say it, get it over with and get your dinner in a doggy bag.*

"I know. It's my family. I'm not going to pretend it's normal. I know it's not."

A child had never been on the radar for Kendall, but

if she was ever going to choose to have a baby, it would
never be like this. With a man she wasn't married to,
from a family that was everything she knew was poison.
She bit down on her lip to keep tears from coming. She
didn't want to cry in front of Sawyer. She didn't want to
cry at all. It so wasn't her style, but her head was such
a jumbled mess right now, it was hard to fight it off.

"See? This is upsetting you. Precisely why I had to
say something."

She dared to look up at him, into his caring and com-
forting eyes. "Why did you have to ask me to dance at
the wedding?"

His vision narrowed. "What?"

"Why couldn't you have just seduced one of the
bridesmaids and left me alone, Sawyer? Everything
would be different now. This wouldn't be such a giant
mess."

"What are you talking about? My father doesn't
know about us. You still would've been working for
me. And as for why I didn't seduce one of the bridesmaids, I didn't want to. I wanted you."

"Why? How am I different from any other woman?"

A breathy laugh rushed from his lips. "Honestly?"

She braced for a comment about her figure, about
how he couldn't stop looking at her breasts.

"You flashed those beautiful blue eyes of yours at me
and I couldn't even see another woman after that. It was
like you'd erased every other woman from that room."

Kendall's breath caught in her chest. That was *not*
the answer she'd been expecting. It would've been so
easy to give in to the romance of it. Sawyer was good

at being smooth. There was no question about that. But eloquent lines and flattery did not add up to much in the end. A single tear rolled down her cheek. It made her so mad at herself. She never should've let him take her to dinner.

"What is going on, Kendall? This is the strangest conversation I've had in a long time, which is saying a lot, considering I had to talk to my father today."

"I'm pregnant and you're the dad." The words popped out of her mouth like a cork from a shaken bottle of champagne.

Sawyer's eyes opened as far as they could. She was racing for something else to say, since it didn't look like Sawyer was going to speak for quite possibly the rest of the evening, just when the waiter beelined for their table with a tray. Dinner.

Neither of them said anything as the food was placed before them. Sawyer might've muttered thank you, but Kendall couldn't be sure. As soon as the waiter was gone, Sawyer turned to her.

"Are you sure?"

"Yes. I'm sure."

"On both counts?"

"That I'm pregnant and the baby is yours?"

"Yes."

"Yes. I'm sure."

The steak sat on Sawyer's plate, untouched. Everything with his dad that day—his whole life—was swirling around in his head like a tornado with no forward momentum, just a powerful vortex that refused to stop spinning. He had no business becoming a dad. None whatsoever. Not with his history. His feelings about institutions like marriage and parenthood were clear in his head—not in the cards for him.

"I don't even know what to say, Kendall. This is a shock, to say the least."

"I know. I deliberated about when to tell you, but I decided there just wasn't a good time."

"Dinner seems like an odd choice."

"Hey. I told you I needed to talk to you in private."

"I couldn't have guessed this was what we would be talking about."

The waiter was chatting with the table next to theirs, then stepped back to them. "Is the meal satisfactory?"

Sawyer picked up his fork and knife and cut into the steak. "Yes. Of course. Just deep in conversation."

The waiter left, and Sawyer took a bite, not enjoying it. He liked Kendall. He liked her a lot. But this was a leap he wasn't prepared to make with any woman.

"You're eating? How can you eat?" Kendall asked.

"What do you want me to do? It's going to seem off if we order and don't eat. The chef is a good friend of mine. If he hears that I came to his restaurant and didn't eat, I'll never hear the end of it. And I *am* hungry."

Kendall shook her head, folded up her napkin and set it next to her plate. She dug her wallet out of her purse, and tucked several bills under the bread basket.

Oh, come on. Seriously?

"Goodbye, Sawyer. I'll talk to you tomorrow. About work." She scooted across the seat and didn't even look at him as she marched out of the restaurant. She wasn't storming, but there was no mistaking this for a leisurely stroll.

He had no choice but to go after her, taking extra-long strides that he hoped wouldn't call attention to the fact that he was chasing a woman out of a restaurant. He caught up to Kendall as she waited at the coat check.

He gripped her shoulder and she whipped around, pulling back. "What?"

"Kendall. Come on. Come back to the table. We'll finish dinner and then we can go somewhere quieter and discuss this. Like adults."

She took her coat and put it on. "It's okay. We don't need to talk about this. Just forget that I ever mentioned it. We'll be done working together after December fifth, and you can go your way and I'll go mine. I don't need your help. You're obviously too shocked to deal with it, but I did think you deserved to know." She turned on her heel and stormed through the door.

Again, he had to follow her. "At least let my driver take you home. And I really think we should talk about this tonight."

"I don't know how many times I need to tell you that I don't need you to give me a ride. I don't need a ride from any member of the Locke family for that matter. I'm perfectly capable of getting home on my own."

"Now it feels like you're just picking a fight. I don't see any reason for you to be mad at me. I've known this new bit of information for all of five minutes. I'm sorry if I'm not yet ready to throw a baby shower or pass out cigars."

Kendall's jaw tensed in a way that he'd never seen

before. Her chin dimpled, her lower lip quivered. "The apple doesn't fall far from the tree, does it? You're just as cold and unfeeling as your father, aren't you? He treats women like they're playthings. So do you. Except you don't marry them, do you? That would be too much like your dad, huh? Is that your way of proving to the world that you're not like him? Because it's not working with me, Sawyer. I see you for what you are and part of me is sorry I ever met you."

Sawyer's usual immediate response when anyone compared him to his father was anger or outrage. But not with Kendall. Not that her words didn't cut. They did. It was just something about her...the sincerity with which she'd ripped him apart, the conviction in her voice, the realization that she had an awful lot to lose by saying those things to him. It would be so easy to fire her. Too easy.

He wouldn't do that to her. She'd earned the job and his respect. *He'd* earned the lecture. He took a deep breath, unsure if the speech he was about to deliver would help anything at all. "I'm sorry. I'm truly sorry. I was shocked by your announcement, but I'd like to have a chance to at least talk to you about it. I'm not a bad guy. I'm really not. I'm definitely not my father. Let me prove that to you."

She looked away, up the street, where the breezy night blew her hair back from her face. That was Kendall in a nutshell—facing the storm, head on, always brave. She turned back to him. "Where should we go?"

"You decide."

"My place. Then if I get mad at you again, I can just

send you home and I won't have to worry about going anywhere."

He laughed quietly. "Fair enough. Wait right here. I'll have the car pulled around."

"Can you get the restaurant to wrap up our dinner? I'm still hungry."

"Of course."

Sawyer's driver had the car around front in a few minutes and they were off to Kendall's apartment, with dinner in a to-go bag from the restaurant. They didn't talk during the drive, but Sawyer sensed that Kendall's anger with him had ebbed. As for what he was feeling, he wasn't sure. He was still in shock. When they arrived, Sawyer sent his driver home for the night and said he would catch a cab when it was time to go.

Kendall's apartment was a third-floor walk-up. "Sorry. It's not anywhere near as nice as your place. But it's home."

He stepped inside as she flipped on the lights and took the carry-out bag from him, setting it on the kitchen counter. A small living room was straight ahead, filled with a mishmash of vintage furniture. Most of it looked like 1960s era. "It's nice. I like seeing where you live. It helps me see you in a new light." It occurred to him that so much of their entire existence as a pair—coworkers and lovers—had revolved around him. His hotel, his apartment.

"Good. I'm glad." She pulled the takeout containers from the bag. "Do you want me to heat anything up?"

Sawyer shook his head. "No. I'm fine."

Kendall put everything on dishes and directed him

over to a small table for two with an aqua-and-gray boomerang-print tabletop and matching upholstered chairs. She opened the fridge and peered inside. "No wine, but I have a beer if you want one."

For the first time in a long time, he didn't want a drink. He didn't want to imbibe alone, but he was also starting to realize that, though he might have been shocked to learn about the pregnancy, her entire life had changed with that piece of information. "I'm fine with water."

Kendall brought two glass tumblers to the table. "Finally. We eat." She took one bite and groaned quietly. "Even room temperature, this is insanely good."

"Told you. Maybe I can take you back there sometime. When there are less serious subjects to be discussed. I really am sorry I didn't listen to you in the first place."

"I should have insisted. It was my fault. I couldn't have expected you to be able to figure out from the tone of my voice just how bad an idea it was."

"Did you find out today?"

She nodded. "I've been so tired. I finally just went to the doctor."

Kendall explained everything the doctor had said about her symptoms and the reasons why her birth control pills must have been less effective. "So yeah. I guess we made a baby that night at the wedding. What are the odds, huh?"

As much as he'd felt like a jerk before, it was so much worse now. If they hadn't ended up running into each other because of work, she would still be pregnant right now, and he never would've known. She likely wouldn't have called him. He knew Kendall by now. She was too proud. "Right. And what are your plans?" He didn't know what else to ask. This was such new territory for him.

"I haven't had time to make plans. Right now, I'm too focused on the Grand Legacy. There's not much I can do except take good care of myself. We'll get past the grand opening, and then I'll start worrying about things like cribs and childcare. I still don't even know if I'm going to get the promotion I want." She stared up at the ceiling. "God. I really hope I get the promotion. It will make life with a baby much easier."

He listened, unable to keep from noticing that nothing she was talking about involved him. "I don't want you to worry about that. Whatever you need, you'll have it from me." His stomach knotted. He knew exactly how that sounded, like he was the wealthy guy taking care of a problem. "I just don't want you to think I won't accept my responsibility." Somehow, that sounded even worse.

Kendall held her finger up to her lips. Her eyes were watery again. "Please stop talking. I don't want to think about any of that right now, okay. We can figure out your role in this some other time. I realize it's an odd predicament, but I don't want it to ruin our professional relationship."

His shoulders dropped and he reached across the table for her hand. "Kendall. Can we just accept the fact that our relationship has gone well beyond the professional? I mean, even if we're letting the world think something else, there's no question that you and I are intertwined now. I don't want to think that we're going to walk away from each other on December sixth."

"I don't want to think that either. But I also don't believe in trapping someone. That doesn't lend itself to happy outcomes. You know?"

He nodded. "I know." He rubbed the back of her hand with his thumb. "I'd like to try, though. I think we're good together. And I'd like to try."

She sucked in a deep breath, and looked into his eyes intently. "This is serious, Sawyer. There is no trying. My heart can't handle you trying."

"Let me stay the night. We'll talk."

She shook her head. "I don't think that's a good idea. We'll just be muddying the waters."

"No sex. I just want to be with you." *I just want you to let me try.*

Thirteen

Sawyer had slept over three nights in a row. No sex. Just talking and sleeping. They talked about the future, about what each of them wanted. They went over the reasons each of them was so completely unsure of what to do, but Sawyer didn't seem to be getting any more comfortable with the idea of a baby. In fact, when Kendall asked him to join her at her first appointment with the obstetrician, it was met with so much hesitation that she didn't bother to push him on it. The problem was that with each passing day of uncertainty from him, Kendall felt herself retreating. Shoring up her defenses. She knew her own tendencies and she knew why they were there—self-preservation. She and Sawyer had unwittingly thrown themselves into a lifelong commitment, and there were exactly

zero easy answers after that. For Kendall, the notion
of relying on Sawyer for anything was in direct opposition to her instincts. It had been her and only her
for so long. She'd trained herself not to count on a
man for anything.

Sawyer left very early that morning and Kendall
made a point of getting to work on time. But something was off from the moment she walked through
the door. Maureen, the receptionist, was on the phone.
She glanced up at Kendall, then averted her eyes. No
smile. Had someone else been fired? Had the firm been
dumped by a client?

Kendall walked down the hall, and it was more of
the same, except now it was hard not to take it person-
ally. People were avoiding eye contact, only muttering
good morning. In fact, she didn't hear a single demon-
strative thing until Wes yelled from his office, "Good
morning, Kendall. Beautiful day, isn't it?"

She stopped dead in her tracks. Something was definitely wrong. She poked her head into his open doorway. "What's going on?"

The smugness in his smile radiated like heat off as-
phalt in summer. "Just working hard. Trying to impress
the boss. You should try it sometime." He dropped the
grin. "Seriously. You should try it."

Kendall wasn't about to stick around for clarification.
She padded lightly into her office. She was just being
paranoid, right? People were busy. They were preoccupied. She opened up her laptop bag and that's when
she saw the note waiting on her desk.

Kendall,
I need to talk to you first thing.
Jillian

The blood in her veins turned to an icy sludge—cold and heavy. Jillian had never before left her a handwritten note. It was always a verbal order left with reception. This wasn't good. She wasn't being paranoid.

Kendall straightened her dress and her spine, leaving her phone behind. As she marched down the hall and turned into the reception area outside the executive offices, she was struck by how much she wanted this job. Intellectually, she'd known she wanted it from the moment it was a possibility. Heck, she'd wanted it before then, when it was remote and unlikely. Walking past the empty VP office, the reminder to everyone that this prized position was up for grabs, Kendall was overcome with territoriality. She wasn't generally like this, but dammit, this was her job.

Jillian's assistant caught sight of Kendall. "Ms. Ross. Jillian wants to see you right away." It sounded like an executioner's decree.

"That's why I'm here." She forced a smile. *Happy people are harder to fire, aren't they?* Into Jillian's office she went, even when her knees felt like rubber and her heart, although working twice as hard as normal, wasn't succeeding in pumping any blood at all.

"Kendall. Close the door, please."

Kendall turned to do as instructed, but Jillian's assistant was already there, doing it for her. *Best to shut out the desperate cries for help, huh?* "You asked to see me?" Kendall remained standing. It would make for a quicker escape.

"I know about you and Sawyer Locke."

Hearing it out loud was like taking a knee to the ribs. She could hardly breathe. She'd thought about the consequences of her actions. She hadn't thought about what the delivery of those consequences would feel like.

"Someone sent me photos," Jillian continued. "I don't know who, but it doesn't matter. It's obvious to me that you have not only crossed the line, it has been going on for a while. And that means there has been an ongoing effort on your part to deceive me. To say that I'm disappointed would be an understatement."

Now she knew how stupid she'd been to base her fear solely on losing her job. Jillian's words were far worse. Kendall had thrown away the trust of her mentor. How could she have done that? Kendall's mind whirred with excuses, none of which were worth a thing. *Just look at him. You try to resist him.* She knew how pointless it all was. And she hated the way Jillian thought of her now, like she didn't put her career first.

"Do you have anything to say for yourself?" she asked.

Except now, there was more than her career to worry about. There was a baby, who would need food and clothes, diapers and a college fund, and most certainly a roof overhead. "Yes. Please let me explain."

"I have zero tolerance for this."

"I know that. But I'm telling you that Sawyer and I

were involved before he even set foot into this office. So it's not quite what you're thinking."

Jillian's focus narrowed. "The first meeting he had in our office? I only got the impression that you knew each other. There was no evidence of romance."

Kendall didn't know exactly how to proceed. She was walking a very narrow line right now. "There wasn't any that day. It was in the past."

"I'm not sure that makes things better. You should have said something." Jillian sat back in her chair, shaking her head from side to side. "I will never understand why a woman is so willing to commit professional suicide because of a man."

"I had no way of knowing he was going to walk into this office."

"Why didn't you tell me the truth? Right then and there."

"Did I even have an opportunity? I had no time to prepare for the meeting, and my primary goal was winning the account. I was not thinking about romance. I was thinking about my job and nothing else." Okay, so that part was a little bit of a fib, but it was mostly true and that was as good as things were going to get today.

"I have to take you off the account. Effective immediately."

Kendall's pulse raced. All that work. All those hours. It meant so much to her. And it meant so much to Sawyer. "No. No. Please don't do that. I've busted my behind on this account. The Grand Legacy is going to be the pinnacle of my PR career so far."

"Sorry. I don't care about the past you and Sawyer

might have. I only care about Sloan PR. And that means the account is going to Wes."

"But…"

"My decision is made." She turned away and began flipping through a stack of papers on her desk.

Does this mean I'm not getting fired? "What about the VP position?"

"It's Wes's to lose now. As far as I'm concerned, you're no longer a candidate."

She wasn't sure of the wisdom of begging, but she had to make a case for herself. "You know I'm perfect for that job."

"You were perfect. Past tense. I can't give it to you now. I'm already being a hypocrite by letting you stay on. Don't forget that I fired Wanda for nearly the same thing."

"Why are you letting me stay?"

"It's not because you're brilliant. It's because I'm too short-staffed right now."

"Oh."

"And if you want to keep the job you already have, stay away from Sawyer Locke. I don't even want to know that you're talking to him on the phone or sending him an email. One word of that and you're done, Kendall. There is no wiggle room, especially not with a client this high profile."

"Yes, ma'am. Of course." Kendall's heart was about to dissolve into nothing. Not only was this everything she deserved, it was everything she feared, all wrapped up in one big depressing package.

"Until then, I want you on your A game. On time

to work. Every day. No more arguments with Wes. I don't want to hear him complain about you even once."

Why don't you just give me an impossible task? "Of course. What do you want me to work on if I'm not working on the Grand Legacy?"

"You'll need to take Wes's smaller accounts to free up his time. Ask him what he wants off his plate."

Kendall's stomach lurched. "Are you saying I report to Wes now?"

"In a way, yes. I don't have time to figure out who's doing what. You two will have to work it out. I definitely want you taking the lead on Yum Yum Dog Food. Wes hates that account. They're impossible to work with."

Great. "Okay. Thank you." Kendall didn't have a choice but to be thankful. She was lucky to get out of Jillian's office with a job of any sort. There was a baby to worry about now, and she was the only person she could count on when it came to taking care of the tiny life growing in her belly.

Sawyer got a text from Kendall. We need to talk. In private. No restaurants.

Last time she'd made this request, she'd told him she was pregnant. What now? Twins? Okay. Where?

My apartment. 6:30? Please be discreet.

Discreet? What in the world was going on? Everything okay?

Not really. But I can't talk about it now.

Sawyer was still wrestling with the pregnancy. He might have reacted poorly, but he couldn't help it. Everything with his dad had put him on edge that day after nearly a lifetime of living with Locke drama. Maybe the Lockes simply weren't cut out for love. His father was good at getting married, but Sawyer wasn't convinced he knew what love was. Noah had shown no ability to be with a woman for more than a few days. His sister, Charlotte, ever the flighty party girl, was off sowing her wild oats in Europe and had been for the last two months. She always had lots of male attention, but rarely a boyfriend. Maybe it was genetic. Maybe the love their mother had shown them was all there ever would be. Not everyone lived a life filled with personal satisfaction, did they? Sawyer had done fine up until now without it. The one time he'd dared to think love or commitment was a good idea, he'd ended up with his heart torn in two. His work, although frustrating at times, never failed him. When his dad wasn't interfering, there were days when he couldn't see any reason to put effort into anything else. And the opening of the hotel? That would be a long-awaited dream come true. Maybe the Grand Legacy, and nothing else, was meant to be his future.

He arrived at her apartment on time, in a cab rather than having his driver take him. He was prepared to try to make Kendall happy, however shaky things were between them. Maybe he'd get to stay for dinner. Maybe he'd get to sleep over. Maybe she'd let him have a night off from the baby discussions and he could have the chance to come to terms with the idea of the pregnancy on his own. He didn't want to shut the door on Kendall, as much as he was entirely uncertain about his ability to make it work, and even more unsure of becoming a dad.

"Hey," she said, answering the door. She had no makeup on, her hair back in a ponytail. She was wearing yoga pants and a big, baggy top. Her feet were bare, but the most striking detail was her eyes. They were crystal clear, but ringed in pink. She'd been crying.

"What's wrong?"

"Just come in." She looked both ways down the hall and closed the door, flipping the latch.

Sawyer got settled while Kendall peeked between the shades and closed them.

"Do you want to tell me what you're doing? I feel like we're in a spy movie."

She perched on the edge of the chair opposite him, her arms wrapped around her waist, closing herself off from him. "Not that far off, unfortunately. I almost got fired today. Jillian found out about us."

"How?"

"Photographs. Someone sent her pictures of me leaving your apartment the morning after your dad tried to bribe me."

"I'm so sorry if it was my dad. I really hope it wasn't." Sawyer shook his head and sat down on the couch. "You know, I understand that most companies don't like the appearance of this sort of thing, but we knew each other before you had the job. That changes things. I don't think it's the same."

"As far as Jillian's concerned, that makes it worse.

She feels like we were colluding that day you came in for the first meeting."

"What about the pregnancy? Did you tell her about that?"

"No, I didn't tell her that. That would just make it more complicated. We're not actually dating, Sawyer. We're not a couple. How would I even explain that?"

"We're having a baby together. It's very simple."

"Are we having a baby together, Sawyer? Because I don't think we are. Especially when I go to the doctor on my own and it's apparently my job to convince you this is a good idea in the first place. When you sleep over every night, just so you can tell me time and time again that you have dozens of reservations about this. It doesn't make me feel good or secure or happy."

The circles he and Kendall had talked themselves into were endless. "And I told you, I never asked for this. If it was my call, I would never become a dad. Ever. It's just not part of the way I see myself."

She closed her eyes and sat back in her seat, pulling her legs up and resting her feet on the edge of the chair. "I'm so glad you have this choice, Sawyer. Really, I am."

"Don't do that. Don't say that. I'm being honest with you, Kendall. What more do you want from me? I can't manufacture a happy response to any of this. And surely you wouldn't want me to make something up."

"Look, I almost got fired today because of you. I almost threw my entire career away so you and I could sleep together a few times."

Her words hurt so much more than Sawyer ever imagined. "That makes it sound so terrible."

"It's all terrible. Every last bit of it. And it only gets worse. Jillian pulled me off your project."

Wow. It really did get worse. Sawyer couldn't fathom moving forward with the Grand Legacy project without Kendall. In fact, there were a lot of things he couldn't imagine without Kendall, but things were going off the rails so quickly, he couldn't keep up. "No. She can't do that."

"She not only can do it, she's done it. You signed a contract with the agency. It doesn't guarantee my involvement. Now you get Wes."

"The guy who gossiped about the engagement ring? I don't want to work with him."

Kendall shrugged. "What do you want me to say? We put ourselves in this terrible situation and we're just going to have to live with it. We knew it was wrong and we did it anyway."

He drew in a deep breath. It was time to fix things. Kendall was excellent at fixing things. He had to show her he could do the same. "I'll go talk to Jillian. Straighten this all out. It'll be fine. I don't want you to worry about it."

The color rose in Kendall's cheeks. "Don't you dare go to my boss about this. I do not need you going in there and sticking up for me. That will destroy any remaining shreds of respect Jillian might have for me. She thinks I'm a woman who's willing to sacrifice her career for a man, and the truth is, Sawyer, I'm not. I'm not that woman. I was fine before you ever came along and I'll be fine without you after you walk out the door."

It felt like his heart was going to hammer its way out

of his chest. "What are you saying?" He was so over-whelmed right now with emotions that were impossible to separate—anger, sadness, regret, uncertainty.

"This has to be over, Sawyer. You don't want to be a dad and I don't want to lose my job. And until you're ready to show me that you're on board with the baby, it's too painful for us to be together." The tone in her voice had become so definitive. So resolute.

Sawyer didn't know what to say. "I don't think you're thinking this through."

"The job was just the final nail in the coffin. I've seen the writing on the wall since the night I told you I was pregnant. I saw it in your eyes. You don't want this. I know you don't. And that's okay. I can't expect you to be excited or thrilled about something that you never asked for. It's not fair to you."

Funny, but as she told him everything he'd been thinking, it occurred to him that it wasn't at all the way he wanted to feel. He wanted to be excited. He wanted to be thrilled by the possibilities. Here was this incredible woman in front of him and she had his child growing inside of her. But he wasn't sure he had it in him to be a dad—a real dad, the kind of dad who reads bedtime stories and takes his kid to the park and shows unconditional love. His uncertainty about his own abilities was his biggest stumbling block. It made him feel like a failure to think it, let alone admit it to Kendall.

"I'm not worried about being fair to me," he said, watching as she got up out of her seat and opened the apartment door. "I won't shirk my responsibilities. You have to know that."

Kendall gestured for him to leave. "I know you won't. I know that much about you, Sawyer. I know you're enough of a stand-up guy to help me pay the rent and buy diapers. That's not the problem." He went to her, but she made it clear with a turn of her shoulder that she didn't want him to touch her. "The problem is I need a man to stick around for longer than it takes to hand out some money."

Fourteen

Sawyer's stomach rumbled and groaned. He shifted in his seat, trying to ignore it, but the PR report he was reading was yet another reminder of everything that was wrong. It'd been two weeks without seeing Kendall and it was slowly killing him. She refused to take his phone calls. There was no way to know if she actually listened to his messages. He was guilty of leaving several.

Yet another grumble rose from his belly. He'd hardly eaten lunch. Food didn't hold much allure right now. Nothing pleasurable held any appeal at all. Not without Kendall. But he had to eat. And he didn't want to do it alone.

"Hey, Noah," he called out to the near-empty office. Like most nights, everyone but he and his brother had gone home at five. It was now after six thirty.

Noah appeared in the doorway, pulling on his coat. "I'm getting out of here. I can't stand another minute behind these four walls."

"Do you have dinner plans? I'm starving."

"Honestly? You look worse than starving. You look like you're dying. You have dark circles under your eyes. Your skin looks like hell and that suit is practically hanging off you."

Sawyer pursed his lips and began to collect his things. "All the more reason for you to take me out to dinner."

"Okay. I'm game."

The brothers made their way downstairs and out onto the street. The chill in the air was unmistakable. Sawyer loved fall—crisp air and football season. Nothing was better than that. It brought to mind the day he and Kendall had spent at his apartment, the day he'd watched her sleep. Even though things had been complicated then, they were still simpler than they were now. It was all before the baby. All before the ugliest parts of him and his past had come to the surface.

"You okay?" Noah asked, hands shoved in his pockets as they marched up Eighth Avenue.

"Yeah. Just hungry. And preoccupied."

They arrived at their destination—one of their favorite spots, an old Irish pub. They sat in their favorite booth and the waitress brought them waters and menus. "What are we drinking tonight?" she asked, with the perfect amount of attitude.

Sawyer loved the presumption. Drowning his sorrows in a beer was right on time. "Pint of Guinness."

"Same for me." Noah perused his menu for a few seconds before closing it. He sat back and draped his arms across the seat. "So are you going to tell me why you're so especially miserable right now or do I have to drag it out of you?"

"We're both under a lot of stress right now. Carrying out Kendall's plan is a lot of work." He didn't go on. It was enough of a miracle that he'd said her name without his voice cracking.

"It's brutal if you ask me, but I love it. Once the hotel is finally open, we can just move forward and start making our money back. No more treading water."

"Right." Except Sawyer couldn't even see beyond the hotel opening. It was like his life narrowed to a dark point on December 5 and there was nothing else beyond that. Well, not exactly nothing, but Kendall had made it clear that until he got on board with the baby, 100 percent, anything between them was a nonstarter. She wasn't about to put up with a halfhearted attempt at making things work between them. She wanted it all.

The waitress delivered their beers and took their orders. Sawyer couldn't put any thought into making decisions right now, so he simply ordered the same club sandwich Noah did. Their food came out quickly and Sawyer had to admit that between the beer and some sustenance, he was starting to feel better. Or if not better, at least more human.

"Okay, now that you've got your blood sugar back up, do you want to tell me what's really going on? Because the stress story only gets you so far. I might be stressed, but I don't look like I've been living under a rock."

Sawyer took another long drink of his beer, but it didn't take away the pain. He didn't know which way was up anymore. But he certainly knew which way was down. "It's the Kendall thing, I guess."

"Yeah. That was a bad way for it to end. That's the cost of getting involved with a Locke, I suppose."

"I guess." Except Sawyer was starting to think it was all a lot of bull. Why was he subscribing to this idea? Simply because things hadn't worked out before didn't mean they would never work out. "No. You know what? That right there is the problem. I hate that thinking."

Noah shrugged. "It is what it is."

"No. I'm not living with that anymore. We might be Lockes, but we're also half our mother. This isn't what Mom would've wanted for us. She wouldn't have wanted our family to be like this."

Sadness crossed Noah's face. "It's easy for you to say that. I don't remember her like you do."

It was indeed true that Sawyer'd had more time with their mother. His memories of her were vivid and real, while he suspected those of Noah and his sister, Charlotte, weren't as vibrant. None of this would be going on at all right now if she were still alive. She'd kept their father in check. She'd kept him grounded. Or at least it had seemed that way, from the vantage point of a little boy. What would she say right now if she knew about the hotel? Or for that matter, what would she say about Kendall and him? About the baby?

A vision popped into Sawyer's head, one that made tears sting his eyes. He never cried, but sitting there in the dark of that bar with his brother, it might happen. His mom would've adored Kendall. His mom had been spirited and didn't take any guff from anyone. And how would she have felt to know she was going to become a grandmother? She would've been full of glee. And maybe that's where the sadness and trepidation was coming from. He couldn't go to his own dad and tell him, "I'm going to be a father. You're going to be a grandpa." There would be no unconditional love or joy in that statement.

That was the real tragedy of the current state of being a member of the Locke family.

"Kendall is pregnant. The baby is mine." Sawyer couldn't keep it inside anymore. He needed someone close to him to know.

Noah's eyes were as big as hubcaps. "Are you sure?"

"Yes, I'm sure. What kind of question is that?" Now Sawyer fully appreciated why that question had made Kendall so angry. It was insulting. How many jerky things could he have possibly said to her? Too many, apparently.

"I'm just asking. People have been known to lie about this sort of thing. Especially when one person has a vast personal fortune on the line."

"Yes, I'm sure. I trust Kendall." The realization quickly followed the words. He hadn't even thought before he'd said them—they'd rolled off his tongue as naturally as could be.

"So what are you going to do?"

"I have no idea. I didn't handle the news well when she told me." Sawyer hated to do it, but he relayed every terrible thing he'd said to her. "I'm not proud of the way I acted."

Noah downed the last of his beer and flagged the waitress, mouthing *two more* and pointing to their empty glasses. "I don't think I would be proud either, and we both know that you are far smoother with the ladies than I am. I'm the one who gets myself into terrible situations."

"So what do I do? I'm really not sure I'm cut out to be a dad. And that is a real dealbreaker for Kendall, as it should be. I told her I could try with her, but she said that wasn't good enough."

"Probably because it's not."

The waitress set down their two beers. "You still working on dinner?"

Sawyer pushed aside his half-eaten plate of food. Noah had demolished his. "I'm good. Thank you."

"I don't know why you say you aren't going to be a good dad," Noah said when the waitress left. "You're practically a dad to me and you're only three years older. I don't know how I could've dealt with growing up in that house if you hadn't been around to talk to."

Sawyer almost couldn't believe what his brother was saying. He'd never once thought of himself that way. If anything, he'd always worried that he leaned on Noah and Charlotte too much, complained too much to them about their dad. "Really?"

"Yes, really. Think about it. Who taught me to ride a bike? You did."

"That's only because the butler taught me to ride a

bike and he was too old to be doing stuff like that in the first place."

"Who talked to me about girls? Who bought me my first box of condoms? Who talked to me about college and about doing my own thing and not living in the shadow of our family name."

Sawyer traced a groove in the surface of the aged wood table with his finger. "I did, I guess."

"There's no guessing. You did those things and I'm thankful to you for it. I'm thankful I have you as my partner. You are a rock, Sawyer. If anyone should be a dad, it should be you."

The words echoed in his head like few anyone had ever said to him. *If anyone should be a dad, it should be you.* "How do I make things better with Kendall? How do I prove that I'm up for this challenge? I'm not sure she'll believe me."

"First off, I've seen the way you look at her. I know you love her."

How Noah saw these things in him that he didn't see in himself were beyond him. Love? Really? "How do you know that?"

Noah rolled his eyes. "If you didn't love her, you wouldn't be so miserable without her. It's not rocket science." He took a swig of his beer. "I know you aren't going to want to hear this, but you have to buy her an engagement ring. You're going to have to ask her to marry you."

Sawyer knew where this led, but it didn't make the idea any easier to take. An engagement ring was a very emotional thing for him. Just the thought of walking into a jewelry store made him uneasy. He also wasn't convinced a ring would be enough for Kendall. She would need more. A lot more.

"I gotta get out of here," Sawyer said, fishing his wallet out of his pocket and slapping a credit card on the table. "I've had too much to drink." He pulled out his phone and sent a text to his driver, asking him to pick him up outside the restaurant.

"Two beers and you're under the table? I thought we were going to spend some time together tonight."

He shook his head and ran his hand through his hair. "That's what happens when you don't eat. It goes straight to your head. Plus, I need to get some sleep if I'm going to get through tomorrow. I have a meeting with Wes about media night." *God help me.*

Sawyer and Noah wandered outside, climbing into Sawyer's car. They dropped Noah at his place, only a few blocks away from Sawyer's.

"You know what, Mike? Can you take me to Kendall's?"

"Certainly, sir."

Sawyer knew it wasn't the right thing to do, but he wanted her so badly he could taste it. And it wasn't the beer talking. It was his gut. Maybe it was time to start listening to his instincts. Maybe it was time to make an emotional decision for once in his life.

He pulled out his phone to call her, but she didn't pick up. Hearing her voice only made the longing for her that much greater. "Hey, Kendall. It's nice to hear your voice. I was just thinking about you. I wanted to see how you're doing. And how you're feeling. It's so strange that I don't know what's going on with you." His head was underwater from the beer, but those last few words out of his mouth were like coming to the surface and getting a gulp of fresh air, only to be pushed back under again. His brother telling him he loved Kendall didn't make it true. It was this feeling he had right now. Like someone had hollowed out his chest.

They pulled up outside Kendall's building. The lights were off. Hopefully, she was getting some rest. Hopefully, it was peaceful. She had to be feeling uncertain about the future. Or maybe she was prepared to tackle what came next all on her own. That would be the most like Kendall. "I wish you would talk to me. I wish you would pick up the phone. I just need to know that you're okay."

He dropped his phone on the seat. "We can head back to the apartment," he said to his driver.

Phone calls were only going to get him so far with Kendall. Words were one thing and action was quite another. He needed to get to work if he was going to win Kendall back. He might have just gone through hell with the remodel of the Grand Legacy, he might be running on almost no sleep, but he needed to start another project. This one at home.

Kendall lay in her bed in the dark not sleeping. A voice mail from Sawyer waited on her phone like a ticking time bomb. She didn't want to go there. But she had to. She still had this bizarre sense of loyalty to him, wrapped up inside a giant mess of a relationship…her career in ruins, a baby on the way, her future entirely uncertain.

It was best to just get it over with. If it made her cry or made her mad or just made her plain old upset, she wouldn't have to endure the emotion for long. She was so tired right now, she would eventually fall asleep, especially after a few tears.

She pushed Play. In the inky blackness of her room, his voice blanketed her with profound longing and sadness, so heavy that it threatened to smother her. His words, the timbre of his voice, it all wore her down, syllable by syllable. *I wish you would talk to me. I wish you would pick up the phone.* And then there was the worst of it—*I just need to know that you're okay.*

She turned onto her side and the tears came, rolling across her nose and onto the pillow. How had everything turned so upside down since the day she'd first put on the engagement ring? It was supposed to protect her. It was supposed to keep her on track. She not only didn't feel safe, she was as far off course as she could've imagined. If she'd tried to anticipate the worst that could happen, she never would've come up with this.

In some ways, it would've been better if Jillian had just fired her. Then Sawyer could truly know the price she'd paid for their time together. Being in limbo left things far too ambiguous. It gave Sawyer an excuse and she didn't want to give him a single one. Not even part of one. He was the golden boy, the wealthy guy who got everything he wanted.

Or was he? She flopped over onto her back and stared up at the ceiling, which she could barely see through the darkness. The truth was that Sawyer wasn't that rich jerk who got whatever he wanted, as much as she'd tried to put him in that pigeonhole. He'd suffered at the hands of his own father, all while trying to do the right thing and live up to his great-grandfather's dreams. He'd been through hell with his ex-fiancée. Money might make life easier, but it didn't give free passes on heartache.

She turned back and flipped on the bedside table light and climbed out of bed. She went to the closet in search of the thing she'd so innocently looked for that fateful morning—the box with the ring. She got it down off the shelf and sat on the edge of her bed. The ring was back in its safe place and Kendall didn't have the strength to even look at it now. It was there and that was all she needed to know. What she really wanted were the pictures.

There weren't many. Most had Kendall's mother ducking out of the frame, putting up her hands to shield her face from the camera. When she was little, Kendall had thought her mom was playing a game or trying to make her laugh, especially when she'd say that she looked horrible. Her mom had always been gorgeous, even with no makeup and little sleep, after she'd been out late with one of her boyfriends. Her mom had a fragility that was always threatening to break through the surface. And it wasn't because she was weak. It was because she was desperate to open her heart to someone she could trust. Was that Kendall? Had she learned these things from her mom?

One thing that came to bother Kendall more than

anything was that her mom never was the one to end it. As bad as it got, she'd never send one of these guys packing. She waited them out, until eventually they'd stop calling her back and showing up. Before Kendall had figured it out, that part of the cycle had confounded her. How could anyone leave her mom? She was so sweet. So generous of spirit. But the truth was that her mom never saw it in herself. She only saw the reasons someone might leave. It's hard to love someone who doesn't love herself.

Was that Kendall's problem? She was, after all, one half her mother—a suitably tragic and flawed person, however beautiful and kind she had been. The other half was her father—a man she never knew, the sort of guy who walks out on a woman with a baby, even when he'd had to have known he was sealing their fate when he did. Was that why she couldn't forgive Sawyer for his doubts about fatherhood? Because she still couldn't forgive her own dad, wherever he was, dead or alive, thirty years later?

Part of her wished she had expressed that to Sawyer more fully, helped him understand the reasons why she had high expectations of a man, but she didn't want to force him into anything. She wanted him to want her and the baby. She wanted him to love her. Because she'd already fallen in love with him. Despite his smooth exterior, he was a caring and soulful man. He was a man of conviction, which was far more than she could say about most people. He stood on his own two feet, often in direct opposition to his father, even when he had so much to lose by doing so. Yes, he'd lost his cool when he'd found out about the pregnancy, but he had a lot of complicated feelings wrapped up in the idea of fatherhood.

She put the photographs away and returned the box to its corner of the closet. Focusing on the way she wished things had turned out, for either her or her mother, wasn't going to get her any closer to what she wanted—a future with some certainty. She'd call Sawyer back if she thought he was on board with the baby, but the reality was he'd only asked about her.

Nearly two weeks after Sawyer had left his last voice mail, Kendall was still having a terrible time getting him or his words out of her head. *I wish you would talk to me. I wish you would pick up the phone. I just need to know that you're okay.* The ball was in her court. There were only so many pleading messages a man could leave and still hold on to his pride.

Kendall had been wrestling with it every day. Was there a way to resume the conversation with Sawyer and still keep her job? Or would that just invite more heartache? Things were bleak right now, toiling away on the Yum Yum Dog Food account and going home to an empty apartment each night, but at least they were predictably so.

Today, like every other day since she'd almost been fired, she was sitting at her desk, chewing on a pencil to keep from screaming. Her office door was open, and she could hear Wes and Jillian arguing about the Grand Legacy. Wes was pleading for his professional life, which wasn't entirely upsetting. It was just that his future was tied to the success of the Grand Legacy right now and it had not been going well.

Tonight was the big media night—twenty carefully chosen writers, an exclusive tour of the Grand Legacy just four days before the reopening. By all reports, Sawyer and Noah had been working their fingers to the bone to get things ready. The problem was, Wes was in over his head. He was a whiz when it came to press releases and schmoozing at cocktail parties. But organizing an event? It was outside his frame of expertise, probably because he wasn't used to taking other people's needs into consideration.

"Wes, you cannot expect my assistant to deal with the caterer for your event. She has enough work of her own. Get your act together," Jillian said.

"I do have my act together. But they keep asking me questions I can't answer, and I'm already dealing with hotel accommodations, transportation... I have some big egos on my hands and they all expect to be treated like royalty. It's a lot to deal with."

"Those are excuses. Just get it done," Jillian said, soon breezing down the hall.

Kendall spun around in her chair, and stared out her window, mindlessly watching pigeons on the rooftop of the next building. She thumped her foot on the floor. She gnawed at her thumbnail. It was driving her crazy to know that there was even a sliver of a chance that Sawyer's event wouldn't go off without a hitch. If she were in charge, there would be zero problems.

She jumped when there was a knock at her door.

She turned and there was the last person she expected to see. Wes.

"I need your help," he said. "You're the only one who's any good at this stuff."

It would have been so easy to rub his face in it, but the truth was that the Grand Legacy meant too much. The project that Sawyer had poured his heart and soul into was too important. "Yes. Of course."

Wes rushed in and dropped a clipboard on her desk. Before Kendall could get in a word edgewise, he was rattling off the laundry list of problems—writers demanding preferential treatment, the caterer complaining that the on-site kitchen wasn't fully up and running as they'd been told it would be.

"Take a deep breath," Kendall said. "It'll be okay. I'll deal with logistics. You deal with the writers."

Wes's shoulders dropped. "Thank you."

"I'd better go talk to Jillian, though. I'm not supposed to be working on this project at all."

"Are you trying to steal my thunder?"

She shot Wes a look. "No. I'm just trying to make sure I don't come close to getting fired again."

Kendall gathered herself and marched to her boss's office. Jillian's assistant was away from her desk, so Kendall poked her head in the door. "Jillian, do you have a minute?"

"Of course."

Kendall sucked in a deep breath and stepped inside, deciding that she had absolutely nothing to lose. "I need to work on the Grand Legacy media night. The firm can't afford for it to be anything less than flawless."

"Wes went to you for help?"

"He did. But even if he hadn't, I would've shown up in your office at some point today, giving this exact same speech. I completely understand why you had to take me off the project. I should have told you up front what was going on. But the truth is that the promotion, the job and Sawyer were all equally important to me and I was afraid of losing any of them. What Sawyer and I had was not a fling. It meant more than that."

"And now?"

"I'm not sure what the future will hold, but that doesn't mean we can't work together. You know that I belong there tonight. I worked my butt off on this project and you should allow me to be there, so I can see my hard work to fruition."

Jillian sat back in her chair, pursing her lips, seeming deep in thought. Calculating. Taking her sweet time. "You're right. This close to the finish line, we have to do what's best for the client. That means you at the Grand Legacy. Tonight."

Fifteen

As he walked into the Grand Legacy an hour before the media event, Sawyer wasn't feeling nervous, nor was he feeling calm. He was more numb to everything at this point. Running on coffee and two or three hours of sleep for the last several weeks had left him feeling empty, but at least he'd made it this far. The project was nearly complete. A few rooms were being finished, there were hundreds of tiny details on the punch list, but they'd be ready for the big party in four days. There would be champagne flowing and guests checking in. There would be credit cards swiped and money finally moving in the right direction. It was everything he'd worked for, but he'd be lying to himself if he said it felt as good as he'd imagined it would. It felt like very little accomplishment at all without Kendall. In fact, it felt flat-out wrong.

He'd stopped leaving her messages almost two weeks ago. He couldn't be the pathetic guy outside her bedroom window, begging for forgiveness. He needed to be a man of action, and that was exactly what he'd been. He had scrapes on his knuckles and flecks of paint in his hair to prove it. He'd been moving out furniture and moving new pieces in. He'd been scraping off feminine wallpaper borders and patching walls. He'd been painting. In the middle of the night, bleary-eyed and exhausted, he'd thought about hiring someone to do it for him, but he'd been unable to do it. When he finished everything and made his overture to Kendall, hopefully before the grand opening party, he wanted her to see that he had done everything with his own two hands.

Noah walked up to him, a wide smile on his face. "I was just in the speakeasy. Everything looks spectacular. You should go up there."

Sawyer was wiped out just thinking about having to talk to Wes. "Yeah. I'll head up in a little bit. I was going to head back to the security office and check on the monitors that were installed today."

Noah shook his head and grasped Sawyer's shoulders. "No. Dude. You need to go up to the speakeasy. Now. Before anyone else gets here. I promise you will be very happy with what you see."

"Unless it's a bed, a dark room and a pair of earplugs, I doubt it."

"If you don't get up there now, you will never forgive yourself. Trust me."

Sawyer had a sneaking suspicion that the shipment of the rare single malt scotch they'd ordered had finally come in, but he decided that a drink was as good a reason as any to scale the grand staircase and get Noah off his back. As he took each step across the plush black carpet with the cobalt blue scrolls, he reminded himself that someday he would look back on this time fondly, especially if everything worked out the way he wanted it to.

When he took the turn into the main speakeasy entrance, his lungs gave way. It was like he'd been holding his breath for weeks, only he hadn't realized it. *Kendall.*

Standing at the bar, with her back to him, he still knew it was her. Her gorgeous red hair, her sumptuous curves and even more than that—her presence. It was like having pure life pumped back into his veins. She turned and her eyes lit up. She smiled softly. She dropped her chin. He didn't remember making the choice to walk to her. It just happened. The parts of him that wanted so badly to have a second chance were now in charge.

"You're here," he said, taking her hand and inhaling her sweet scent.

"I am." She stepped closer, making the attraction between them impossible to ignore. It was like she was the magnet and he was a hunk of metal.

"On time, no less."

"Technically, I'm early." She licked her lip and bounced her eyebrows.

God, he'd missed her. Every last thing about her. He didn't ever want to let her out of his sights. "What happened?"

"Wes needed help. I couldn't let anything go wrong. It means too much to you."

"After everything? After the way I reacted?" He very much needed to know if she was there to save him or her job. Or both. Or perhaps, there was something else to it. He had a deep need to pull her into his arms and apologize, kiss her, tell her he wanted to try again. That he had been trying this whole time, behind the scenes, especially since he and Noah had their heart-to-heart.

"I can't even believe you're asking those questions. Of course, after everything. The Grand Legacy means a lot to you. Therefore, it means a lot to me. There's no separating the two."

Was that really the way she felt? He looked at her, their gazes connecting, his mind whirring. He'd planned out what to say when the time came to ask big questions of Kendall, but he hadn't thought it would be tonight. "But we are separate right now. And I don't want it to be like that. I really don't."

She shook her head, and raised her finger to her lips. "I know, Sawyer. I got your messages."

"And you never called me back."

"I was saving my hide at work. You know that."

He fought the disappointment threatening to overwhelm him. "And now? Is tonight about saving your job?" He wrapped his fingers around hers, even when he wasn't sure she wanted him to.

She sighed and looked down at their joined hands. "I think we both know there's something between us that could be far more important than either of our careers.

I think we owe each other the chance to talk about it. We owe each other the conversation."

A chance. That was all he needed. "I couldn't agree more. I just want to know that we can have that conversation tonight."

She smiled. "I owe you that much. I owe us that much."

Wes barged into the room seconds later, and Sawyer and Kendall were forced to part and resume their professional roles. Still, that conversation left Sawyer feeling like he'd just slept for a day, had a shot of B12 and could leap tall buildings. All he needed was one more chance.

Kendall and Wes went off to deal with details and arriving writers while Sawyer and Noah went over the plan for the tour and which one of them would be leading which parts. All too soon, the room was filled with their media VIPs enjoying cocktails and food, asking countless questions, vying for the attention of both Sawyer and Noah. Sawyer was immersed in the process and loved talking about the Grand Legacy and his hard work, but he knew very well that he wouldn't be "on" right now if it wasn't for Kendall. If she hadn't swept in, he would be dragging right now. She'd saved the day in more ways than she probably even imagined.

Noah led the beginning of the tour, starting at the top floor with the luxury condominiums that would soon be listed for sale. Next were the three most impressive suites in the hotel, including the one Sawyer and Kendall had christened the day of his interview with Margaret Sharp. As Noah rattled off the list of famous people who had once stayed in this room, she stood in the corner, exchanging glances with Sawyer, charging every atom in his body with her particular brand of electricity. If only she knew what it was like to be on the receiving end of one of her looks—she filled him with optimism and warm feelings he hadn't known in a long time, even when he was unsure everything would work out.

When the group returned to the ground floor, Sawyer led the tour through the finer details of the lobby, then they ended up in the grand ballroom. This was where things had started to come together for Kendall and him—he'd seen the appreciation in her eye and he could see it now. She respected the work he'd done. She admired his dedication. It felt so good to be appreciated for those things.

"I just want to thank everyone for coming this evening. I do hope that those of you who are based in New York will consider coming back in a few days for our big opening night."

Kendall stepped forward and raised her hand. "I want to say one thing before everyone disperses. I hope that the one takeaway everyone has from this evening is that Sawyer and Noah Locke have done everything in their power to bring back a historic piece of this city. They have done so in meticulous fashion, even when faced with setbacks." She cast her eyes across the room at Sawyer. "Too few people put that much care into preserving the past. I think it's something to be admired. Thank you all for coming this evening and giving us your time."

The writers settled in to chatter back and forth, several approaching Kendall and Wes, shaking hands. Sawyer had his own goodbyes to bid, as well, but soon enough, everyone had gone. The caterers and a few members of the newly hired hotel staff were cleaning up the ballroom when finally Sawyer could speak to Kendall alone.

"Thank you so much for everything tonight. I couldn't have done this without you."

Kendall shrugged. "Wes would've muddled his way through it. The food might have not been right, but the hotel looks fantastic. That part would have been in place."

Sawyer shook his head and took her hand. "No, Kendall. It's all you. Just seeing you tonight was enough to put me back on my game. I feel like I've been floundering for the last several weeks."

She nodded, taking in his words. "I haven't been doing great either. But maybe we needed this time to clear our heads. Figure out what we both want."

"Right now, all I want is for you to let me take you home." He hoped like hell she would let it become *their* home. Their family's home.

"Something tells me you won't let me say no."

"You're right. I won't."

Kendall wasn't sure this was the right decision, but the earnest look in Sawyer's eyes left her with no response other than "Are we talking your place or mine?"

"Mine, if that's alright with you."

"I know you're not a big fan of my neighborhood."

"It's more than that. I made some changes to my apartment that I want you to see."

"Changes? How could you have time to do anything other than collapse in bed every night?"

He was quiet for a moment. "I've been a busy guy. I had to keep my mind occupied somehow. I put up some new paint. Got some new furniture." He tugged on her hand. "Come on. Let's go before Noah finds me and asks me to do something."

Kendall grabbed her coat and they rushed outside to Sawyer's waiting car. They sped along in the New York night, no more words to be said, not in the car, where his driver might hear them. If they were going to launch into yet another discussion about the future, it was better to be alone. But there was something about Sawyer tonight. A calm that hadn't been there before. Perhaps it was the product of being so close to the end of the Grand Legacy project. That had to be a huge weight off his mind.

He reached across the seat and placed his hand on Kendall's. It wasn't sexual or seductive, even though there was a rush of excitement every time he touched her. It was sweet and tender. She didn't say anything. She simply turned her hand, so they could be palm-to-palm, so his body heat could pour into her.

They arrived at his building and rode the elevator to his apartment. Sawyer held her hand the whole way, which filled Kendall with both nervousness and exhilaration. Had he decided that he wanted to play a role in the baby's life? And if so, how did that include them as a pair? She didn't want to do any of this halfway, but she recognized now that she could compromise if she had to. The baby wasn't just hers. It was Sawyer's, as well.

He took her coat once they reached his floor.

"So? The big changes?" she asked, looking around, not seeing so much as a throw pillow out of place.

"I'll show them to you in a minute. Can I get you a glass of water? Some tea? You must need to sit down. You've been on your feet all night."

She cocked an eyebrow at him. "It's sweet when you show concern for the pregnant woman."

He took her hand again. "I have always been concerned about you. You know that, don't you? Even when I wasn't taking the news of the pregnancy well. I don't know if I was just losing my mind because of everything going on with the hotel or the drama with my father, but I need you to know that's not me."

"I know, Sawyer. I do. You just never planned to become a father. I get it. We've been down this road."

He shook his head. "Come. Sit." He led her to the living room, clicked on the fire, and they sat together on the couch. "I have spent a lot of my life trying to do everything I could to be the opposite of my dad. I refused to work with him after college, and instead went into the military. I wouldn't work with him when I returned from serving overseas. I went to work right away on building my business so I could afford to bring back the Grand Legacy. Everything I've done has been in opposition."

"I know. You have your reasons."

"But here's where I messed up. It's one thing to not want to be him. It's something completely different when that gets in the way of my happiness. When it prevents me from having the life I want. I never planned on becoming a dad because I simply refused to consider it. But the more I've thought about it, the more I realize that there's this hole in my heart and it's only felt full one time in my entire life."

Kendall swallowed, bracing for the answer. Her heart hoped like crazy that he was about to say what she wanted him to say, but she didn't want to endure more disappointment. "Tell me."

"With you. That first day you came to the hotel, even when I thought I couldn't have you, you still made my world better. You valued what I do, you admired what I wanted to get out of the hotel. You made me feel like somebody, somewhere was on my side. I have never felt like that, Kendall. Never."

"What about with Noah? You work with him every day. You're on the same side."

"That's different. We're bound by blood and money. It's not the same. I know you were just doing your job, but I sensed from the beginning that it meant more to you. And you just confirmed that tonight. I'm so sorry that I ever hurt you. I'm so sorry that I doubted that the baby could make me happy. I know now that you're what makes me happy."

Tears stung her eyes, but she fought back that urge to cry. The truth was that Sawyer made her happy, too. And all of that other stuff was just stuff. Things that would have to get worked out. He made her feel safe. He made her feel protected and cherished. Something she'd only had a glimpse of in her life, and something she'd been so desperate to have again. "You make me happy, too. You do."

"I love you, Kendall. I think I've been in love with you for a while now."

She'd never heard those words from a man before and they sounded so perfect coming from Sawyer's lips. She'd also never thought she'd have the chance to return them, but she knew now that it was right. "I love you, too."

He smiled and rubbed her chin with his thumb. "You do?"

She nodded enthusiastically. "I do."

He leaned forward and placed a soft kiss on her lips. "Perfect. Because now I want to show you the new bed I bought."

She laughed quietly, but they had other issues to address. "Sawyer. We can't just say I love you and have sex and make everything better. We need to discuss the baby. I need to know that you really want to be a dad. That you aren't just saying you do so that we can be together."

He stood and tugged on her arm. "Come on. Just let me show you. You can keep your clothes on."

She followed him down the hall, but he stopped short of his room and opened the door to the guest room—the one that had been girly and feminine. Sawyer flipped on the lights and Kendall felt all of the air from her lungs rush past her lips. Of the many times Sawyer had bowled her over by showing her an impressive room, nothing could top this.

"You made it into a nursery." She surveyed the room,

which was now a lovely pale green. There was a white crib and matching rocking chair. There was a large set of shelves with books and stuffed animals sitting on them, waiting.

"It still needs some work. I didn't want to pick out the crib bedding without you. And if you want to paint it a different color when the baby arrives, we can do that."

She shook her head and held her finger to his lips. The tears started and there was nothing she could do to stop them. They were the product of pure love. "No. It's perfect. It's absolutely perfect." She still couldn't believe he'd done this. "How did you even have time to have this done? With everything going on at the hotel."

"I stayed up all night, every night. I've literally had about six hours of sleep in the last week. I did it all myself. The painting. I assembled the crib."

"You did all of this yourself? Why didn't you just hire someone?"

He pulled her into a hug. "Because this is the sort of thing a dad does for his child."

He and his words were going to be the death of her. He was so sweet, it made her heart ache. "You did an incredible job. But…"

"But what?"

"But what does this mean, Sawyer? Are you asking me to live with you?"

He took both of her hands. He squeezed them. It felt like the whole world had stopped spinning. "I am." He then dropped to his knee.

Kendall yanked one of her hands back, if only to cover her mouth. "What are you doing?"

"I'm asking you to live with me and parent with me and love me. I'm asking you to let me love you and take care of you and let me put a proper engagement ring on your finger. I'm asking you to marry me."

Kendall knew her response, but it was hard to get the words out when she was crying so hard. She nodded quickly. "Yes," she managed to gurgle.

Sawyer got up and opened the top drawer of the bureau next to the crib. He turned with a black velvet box in his hand. He opened it, presenting her with a beautiful solitaire diamond ring. It glinted in an entirely different way than her mom's ring did, probably because she knew what an engagement ring meant to Sawyer. It must have taken a lot for him to buy it. He had to bury his past to do it.

"It's stunning," she said as he slipped it onto her finger. "I love it." She smiled, wondering if this was all real. She had convinced herself this scenario wasn't for her. Now she knew it was because she'd never met the right guy.

"Good. Because I love it, too. It feels so good to know you're wearing that ring for all the right reasons."

Epilogue

It was December 5 and it was snowing. Fluffy white flakes drifted down through the night sky, set against the stunning backdrop Sawyer had waited more than fifteen years to see—the Grand Legacy Hotel all lit up, back to her former glory.

Kendall, arm hooked in his, chattered in the cold. "It's incredible, Sawyer. You must be so proud."

He put his arm around her and pulled her closer to keep her warm, kissing the top of her head. "I am. I really am." Proud didn't begin to express what he was feeling right now. He was filled to the hilt with a sense of accomplishment he couldn't quite explain. This building meant so much more to him than eighteen floors of guest rooms and condos, far more than the ceiling of the grand ballroom and the meticulous details of the speakeasy. It meant there was family history he could tie himself to, that didn't come with the baggage of his father. He didn't have to be defined by the Locke name. He could be defined by the Grand Legacy and everything he'd done to bring it back to life.

"I owe a lot of this to you, though. I couldn't have done it without you."

Kendall shrugged and popped up onto her tiptoes to kiss him on the cheek. "All in a day's work." She'd not only done a fantastic job on the hotel, she'd done a miraculous job on her boss. The day after Sawyer proposed, Kendall marched into work, told Jillian about the baby and said she hoped that being engaged to a soon-to-be former client would be acceptable. Kendall also promised her an invitation to the wedding. Jillian agreed. "Now let's go inside. I'm freezing."

They strolled up to the front doors, opened by two doormen in re-creations of the original uniforms—the finest black wool with gold braid and shiny buttons. As they swept inside, Sawyer was again overcome with optimism and the good memories. The marble floor, with the black granite inlays and silver accents, was back to its original glory. The check-in desk gleamed in black lacquer. He and Kendall were immediately accosted by well-wishers as people milled about and had their picture taken by a photographer Kendall had hired. He was so proud to introduce her to his friends and business associates, proud to have her show off the engagement ring on her finger and reveal with a gentle pat to her belly that she was expecting their child.

Noah and Lily came down the hall from the grand ballroom. "There he is, the man of the hour," Noah said.

Sawyer shook his head, partly because Noah had worked as hard as he had, and also because Noah should not have brought Lily as his date. He'd said it was just business, but Sawyer had heard that excuse before. And he knew that despite the intentions of most people, it didn't always end up working out that way. "We did it," Sawyer said.

"Yes, we did."

"Any sign of Dad tonight?" Sawyer asked, wondering what exactly had compelled him to invite his father after everything that had happened. Perhaps it had simply been his desire to prove to his dad, once and for all, that carrying through with the Grand Legacy project wasn't about defying him. It was about seeing out a promise he'd made to a man who was no longer here to enjoy it. Plus, Sawyer knew to his very core that the hotel would never tarnish the family. In some ways, Sawyer was now able to put his own shine on the Locke name, between the hotel and the baby on the way.

"I doubt we'll see him," Noah said. "But I think that's for the best at this point."

"Agreed." *One mountain at a time.*

"Shall we head up to the speakeasy?" Kendall asked. "I'd love to take a load off and toast to the hotel. With ginger ale, of course."

Sawyer smiled and pressed a kiss to her temple. "Yes."

They left their things with the coat check and began to climb the grand staircase. Sawyer was seeing this part of the hotel in an all-new light, with people bustling all around and enjoying themselves. Fresh paint and hard work were one thing—what the hotel had needed more than anything was life. He couldn't escape the parallels between himself and the hotel, probably because they were so inexorably bound together. New life was what he'd needed to bring himself back from the lonely existence he'd had before. And it arrived in the form of Kendall and their baby. The blessings were too many to comprehend.

They walked into the speakeasy, which was packed with people, nearly wall-to-wall. Jazz played in the background, but it was hard to hear above the roar of conversation. As much as Sawyer had looked forward to this evening, he couldn't wait to put it behind him, take Kendall home and get her out of the gorgeous ivory beaded dress she was wearing. It showed off her curves and her peachy skin in a way that was both maddening and enticing.

From across the room, a woman squealed his name. "Sawyer!"

"Oh, Charlotte's here. She just flew in. Forgot to tell you that," Noah said. "I'm going to grab us some bubbly so we can make a toast."

Through the crowd, Sawyer saw a hand waving in the air, and a few glimpses of Charlotte's long, blond hair as she wound her way past people. She nearly tripped her way out of a tight spot between two couples. For a woman who was known for dancing the night away, Charlotte wasn't particularly graceful.

He embraced his sister. It felt good to have her in his arms. It made it feel as though the whole family was here, even if it was only the three of them. "I'm so glad you made it."

"I wouldn't miss this for the world."

"I want you to meet my fiancée, Kendall." God, that sounded better every time he said it.

Charlotte let out a peal of delight and pulled Kendall into a hug. "I'm so excited I'm going to have a sister. Are you living at Sawyer's now? We'll have to spend some time getting to know each other."

Kendall smiled wide. "Oh, um…" She glanced at Sawyer, telling him he needed to step in.

"Yeah, about the guest room. We turned it into a nursery. I'm so sorry."

Charlotte jutted out her lower lip. "That is the sweetest thing ever. I'm going to be an aunt." She patted Sawyer on the shoulder. "You're going to be the best dad. I just know it."

"We can put you in a room here at the hotel. I hope that will work."

"Actually, that's perfect. Aunt Fran is coming in from England in a few days. She wants to be here for Christmas. She and I can room together."

"Even better. I'll put you two in a suite."

"That would be great. I also want to talk to you about the listings on the condos when you have a chance. Now that I'm back in the city, I need to get serious about real estate again."

Sawyer's head was swimming. Charlotte was always a whirlwind. "Yeah. Fine. Give me a few days. Right now, I need time to sleep and breathe."

Charlotte caught sight of someone on the other side

of the room and waved. "Sounds good. I see some friends from college. I'll find you guys in a little bit." In a flash, Charlotte was gone.

"Sorry," Sawyer said. "She can be a bit much. She has a lot of energy. She always has."

Kendall only smiled. "She's wonderful. I'm an only child. I'm looking forward to having a sister."

Noah returned with a pair of champagne flutes. "I'm just delivering drinks. Ginger ale for Kendall. I promised Lily we'd hunt down some crab cakes downstairs in the grand ballroom."

"Thanks," Sawyer said. "We'll catch up with you two later."

As soon as Noah was gone, Sawyer took Kendall's hand and led her over to the booth in the far corner, which he'd had marked as reserved. They sat on the same side, shoulder to shoulder, with a stunning view of the night sky through the now-restored round window. The snow continued to fall, a little heavier now. In a room bustling with celebration, Sawyer felt a peace he'd never imagined. He clinked his glass with Kendall's. "To the Grand Legacy."

"To love," Kendall countered.

He turned and looked deeply into her blue eyes, thinking he didn't ever want to be anywhere but with her. "To our baby." He took a sip and kissed her softly, the sweet taste of ginger ale still on her lips.

"To our family, Sawyer."

"To our family."

* * * * *

Don't miss Charlotte Locke's story,
available November 2017.
If you loved this story by Karen Booth,
pick up her other romances
from Harlequin Desire:

THE TEN-DAY BABY TAKEOVER
THE BEST MAN'S BABY
THE CEO DADDY NEXT DOOR
PREGNANT BY THE RIVAL CEO
THAT NIGHT WITH THE CEO

Read on for a sneak peek of
DOWN HOME COWBOY
by New York Times *bestselling author*
Maisey Yates.
When rancher and single dad Cain Donnelly
moves to Copper Ridge, Oregon, to make a fresh
start with his teenage daughter, the last thing
he wants is to risk his heart again. So why can't he
keep his eyes—or his hands—off Alison Davis,
the one woman in town guaranteed to
complicate his life?

"HEY, BO," CAIN CALLED, looking around the kitchen and living room area for his daughter, who was on the verge of being late for her second week on the job. "Are you ready to go?"

He heard footsteps hit the bottom landing, followed by a disgusted noise. "Do you have to call me that?"

"Yes," he said, keeping his tone serious. "Though I could always go back to the full name. Violet Beauregarde the Walking Blueberry." She'd thought that nod to *Charlie and the Chocolate Factory* was great. Back when she was four and all he'd had to do was smile funny to get her to belly laugh.

"Pass."

"I have to call you at least one horrifying nickname a week. All the better if it slips out in public."

"Is there public in Copper Ridge? Because I've yet to see it."

"Hey, you serve the public as part of your job at the bakery."

"The presence of humanity does not mean the presence of culture."

"Chill out, Sylvia Plath. Your commitment to being angry at the world is getting old." He shook his head, looking at his dark-haired, green-eyed daughter, who was now edging closer to being a woman than being that round, rosy-cheeked little girl he still saw in his mind's eye.

"Well, you don't have to bear witness to it today. Lane is giving me a ride into town."

Cain frowned. He still hadn't been in to see Violet at work. In part because she clearly didn't want him to. But he had assumed that once she was established and feeling independent she wouldn't mind if he took her to Pie in the Sky.

Apparently, she did.

"Great," he said. "I have more work to do around here anyway."

"The life of a dairy farmer is never dull. Well, no, it's always dull. It just never stops." Violet walked over to the couch where she had deposited her purse yesterday and picked it up. "Same with baking pies, I guess."

"Are you ready to go, Violet?" Lane came breezing into the room looking slightly disheveled, Cain's younger brother Finn closely behind her, also looking suspiciously mussed.

Absolutely no points for guessing what they had just been up to. Though he could see that Violet was oblivious. If she had guessed, she wouldn't be able to hide her reaction. Which warmed his heart in a way. That his teenage daughter was still pretty innocent about some things. That she was still young in some ways.

Hard to retain any sort of innocence when your mother abandoned you. And since he knew all about parental abandonment and how much it screwed with you, he was even angrier that his daughter was going through the same thing.

"Ready," Violet responded.

Even though it was a one-word answer, it lacked the edge usually involved in her responses to him. He supposed being jealous of his brother's girlfriend was a little bit ridiculous.

"Have fun," he said, just because he knew it would irritate her.

He had lost the power to make her laugh. To make her smile, with any kind of ease. So, he supposed he would just embrace his ability to irritate.

At least he excelled at that.

He could tell he had excelled yet again when she didn't smile at him as she left the room with Lane.

"Wait," Finn said, walking past him and grabbing Lane around the waist, turning her and kissing her deep.

It was all Cain could do to keep from groaning audibly. Between his horndog younger brothers and his incredibly happy other brother, he felt like sex was being thrown in his face constantly. Except not in a fun way that involved him having it.

Lane and Violet left, and Finn walked back into the living room. "I'm going to marry that woman," he said, the self-satisfied grin on his face scraping at Cain's current irritation.

"Have you asked her yet?"

"Not officially. But I'm going to. I want to spend the rest of my life with her."

"That's a long time. Trust me. Married years are different than regular years." He had way too much experience living with somebody who didn't even like him anymore. Way too much experience walking quietly through his own house so that he could avoid the conversation that needed to be had, or avoid the silence that seemed magnified when the two of them were in the same room.

He didn't think Finn would suffer the same fate, though. Finn and Lane had known each other for years, and they had been friends before they were a couple. Cain and Kathleen had been stupid and young. He had gotten her pregnant and wanted to do the right thing, instead of doing the kind of thing his father would do.

All in all, it wasn't the best foundation for a marriage.

For a while, they had tried. Both of them. He wasn't really sure when they had stopped.

"I hope you're right," Finn said, obnoxiously cheerful. "I hope every year with Lane feels like five. Because my time with her has been the best of my life."

Given the way they had grown up, Cain really didn't begrudge Finn his happiness. He was glad for his brother, in a way. When he wasn't busy feeling irritated by his own celibate status.

Though, in fairness to him, figuring out how to conduct a physical relationship while he was raising a teenage girl was pretty tricky. He had to set some kind of example. And casual sex wasn't exactly the one he was aiming for.

"Good for you," he said, sounding more annoyed than he had intended.

"How's the barn coming along?"

Cain was grateful for the change in subject. "It's coming."

"Show me."

His brother grabbed his hat off the shelf by the door, and Cain grabbed his own. Strange how this had become somewhat natural. How sharing a space with Finn, Alex and Liam—while annoying on occasion—was just starting to be life.

He took the steps on the front porch two at a time, inhaling the sharp, clear air. It was late summer, and in Texas about now walking outside would be like getting wrapped in a wet blanket. That was also on fire. He could honestly say he didn't miss that part of his adopted home state.

The Oregon coast ran a little cold for his taste, but he had to admit it was still nicer than sweltering. The wind whipped up, filtering through the pine trees and kicking up the smell of wood, hay and horse. If green had a smell, it would be that smell that rode the coastal air across the mountains. Fresh and heavy, all at the same time.

It was fastest to take a truck out to the old barn on the property, the one that had originally stood near the first house that had been built when their great-grandparents had bought the land. The house was long gone, but the barn still remained, and with all of his near-nonexistent free time, Cain had been fashioning the place into a house for Violet and himself.

After they parked, he and his brother walked through the still overgrown pathway that led up to the old barn.

"Wow," Finn said, stepping deeper into the room. "You've done a lot."

"New wiring," Cain said, gesturing broadly. "Insulation, Sheetrock. I need to work on interior walls. But, yeah, it's coming along. It will be fine for the two of us for the next couple of years. And when Violet leaves..."

Unbidden, an image of the beautiful redhead he had seen across the bar last night filtered into his mind's eye. Yeah, in a couple of years he would have a place to bring a woman like that.

Not that he couldn't go back to her place, or get a hotel, but he didn't want to have to explain his absence to a teenage girl who barely thought of him as human, much less wanted to realize he was actually just a guy with a sex drive and everything. Both of them would probably die from the humiliation of that.

"It'll be a pretty nice place," Finn said, and Cain was grateful his younger brother couldn't read his mind.

"Not bad. I know that I could pay somebody to finish it. But right now I'm kind of enjoying the therapy. I spent a long time managing things. Managing a big ranch, not actually working it. Managing my marriage instead of actually working at it. I'm ready to be hands-on again. This is the life that I'm choosing to build for myself. So I guess I better build it."

He knew that at thirty-eight his feelings of midlife angst were totally unearned, but having his wife leave had forced him into kind of a strange crisis point. One where he had started asking himself if that was it. If everything good that he was going to do was behind him.

So, he had left the ranch in Texas—the one he had

spent so many years building up—walked away with a decent chunk of change, and packed his entire life up, packed his kid up, and gone to the West Coast to find… Something else to do. Something else to be. To find a way to reconnect with Violet.

So far, he'd found ranch work and little else. Violet still barely tolerated him in spite of everything he was doing to try to fix their lives, and he didn't feel any closer to moving forward than he had back in Texas.

He was just moved.

Finn's phone buzzed and he pulled it out of his pocket to check his texts. "Hey," he said, "can you pick up Violet tonight from work?"

"I thought Lane was doing it."

"It's her girls' night thing. She forgot."

Well, he had just been thinking that he needed to actually see where Violet worked. "Sure. Sounds good."

"What are you going to do until then?"

"I figured I would do some work in here."

Finn pushed his sleeves up, smiling. "Mind if I help?"

"Sure," Cain said. "Grab a hammer."

ALISON STARED AT the sunken cake sitting on the kitchen countertop and frowned. Then quickly erased the frown so that Violet wouldn't see it.

"I don't know what happened," Violet said, looking perturbed.

"You probably took it out too early. It's nothing a little extra icing can't fix. And it's my girls' night tonight, so I think it can be of use in that environment rather than being put up for sale."

Violet screwed up her face. "It's ugly."

"An ugly cake is still cake. As long as it doesn't have raisins it's fine."

"Oh, I didn't put any raisins in it."

Alison was slightly amused that her newest employee seemed to know about her raisin aversion, even if she didn't quite have cooking times down. Violet was a good employee, but she had absolutely no experience baking. For the most part, Alison had put her on the register, which she had picked up much faster than kitchen duties. But she tried to set aside a certain amount of time every shift to give Violet a chance to get some experience with the actual baking part of the bakery.

Maybe it wasn't as necessary to do with a teenager who had her first job as it was to do with some of the other women who came through the shop, desperately in need of work experience after years out of the workforce, but Alison was applying the same principles to Violet as she did to everyone else.

Right now she was short on staff, and even shorter on people who had the skill level she required with the baked goods to do any training. So while she could farm out Violet's register training, the cakes, pies and other pastries had to be done by her.

"I'll do better next time," Violet said, sounding determined. Which encouraged Alison, because Violet hadn't sounded anything like determined when she had first come in looking for work. Violet was a sullen teenager of the first order. And even though she most definitely made an attempt to put on a good show for

Alison, she was clearly in a full internal battle with her feelings on authority figures.

Having been a horrific teenager herself, Alison felt some level of sympathy for her. But also very little patience. Fortunately, Violet seemed to react well to her brand of no-nonsense response to attitude.

"You will do better next time," Alison said, "because I can eat one mistake cake, but if I have to continue eating them, my jeans aren't going to fit and then I'm going to have to buy new jeans, and that's going to have to come out of your paycheck."

She patted Violet on the shoulder then walked through the double doors that led from the kitchen and behind the counter. The shop was in its late-afternoon lull. A little too close to dinner for most people to be stopping in for pieces of pie.

A rush of air blew into the shop and Alison looked up just in time to see a tall, muscular man walk in through the blue door. A pang of recognition hit her in the chest before she even got a good look at him. She didn't need a good look at him. Because just like the first time she'd seen him, on the other side of Ace's bar, the feeling he created inside of her wasn't logical, wasn't cerebral. It was physical. It lived in her, and it superseded control.

For somebody who prized control, it was an affront on multiple levels.

He lifted his head and confirmed what her jittering nerves already knew. That beneath that dark cowboy hat was the face of the man who had most definitely been looking at her at the bar the night before.

He hadn't left town. He hadn't been a hallucinogenic expression of a fevered imagination. And he had found her.

The twist of attraction turned into something else, just for a moment. A strange kind of panic that she hadn't confronted for a long time. That somehow this man had found out who she was, had tracked her down.

No. That's not it. Even if he did, that doesn't make him crazy. It doesn't.

And more than likely he was just here for a piece of pie. She took a deep breath, steeling herself to look directly at him. Which was... Wow. He was hotter than she remembered. And that was saying something. She had first spotted him in the dim light of the bar, with a healthy amount of space between them.

Now, well, now the daylight was bright, and he was very close. And he was magnificent. The way that black T-shirt hugged all those muscles bordered on obscene, his dark green eyes like the deep of the forest beckoning her to draw close. Except, unlike the forest, his eyes didn't promise solitude and inner peace. No, it was something much more carnal. Or maybe that was just her aforementioned overheated imagination.

His jaw was covered by a neatly trimmed dark beard, and she would normally have said she wasn't a huge fan, but something about the beard on him was like flaunting an excess of testosterone. And she was in a very testosterone-starved state. So it was like stumbling onto water in a desert.

Of course, all of that hyperbole was simply that. His eyes weren't actually promising her anything; in fact, his expression was blank. And she realized that while he might look sexier to her today than he had that night, she might look unrecognizable to him.

Last night she had been wearing an outfit that at least hinted at the fact that she had a female figure. And she'd had makeup on. Plus, she'd gone to the effort to straighten her mass of auburn hair. Today, it was its glorious frizzy self, piled on top of her head, half captured in a rubber band, half pinned down with a pen. And as for makeup... Well, on days when she had to be at the bakery early, that was just not a happening thing.

Her apron disguised her figure, and beneath it, the button-up striped shirt that she had tucked into her jeans wasn't exactly vixen wear.

"Can I...? Can I help you?" She tucked a stray strand of hair behind her ear and found herself tilting her head to the side, her body apparently calling on all of the flirtation skills it hadn't used since she was eighteen years old.

Very immature, underdeveloped skills.

Suddenly, her lips felt dry, so she had to lick them. And when she did, heat flared in those forest green eyes that made her think maybe he did recognize her. Or, if he didn't, maybe his body did. Just like hers recognized his. *Oh, Lord.*

"Yes," he said, his voice much more...taciturn than she had imagined it might be. She hadn't realized until that moment that she had built something of a narrative around him. Brooding, certainly, because he had most definitely been brooding in the bar, but she had imagined he might flirt with a lazy drawl. Of course, it was difficult to tell with one word, but his voice had been clipped. Definitely clipped.

"I have a lot of different pies. I mean, a lot of different kinds. So, if you need suggestions…or a list… I can help."

"I'm not here for pie. I'm here to pick up my daughter…"

Pick up DOWN HOME COWBOY,
the latest COPPER RIDGE novel
from Maisey Yates and HQN Books!

#2533 THE CEO'S NANNY AFFAIR
Billionaires and Babies • by Joss Wood

When billionaire Linc Ballantyne's ex abandons not one, but *two* children, he strikes up a wary deal with her too-sexy sister. She'll be the nanny and they'll keep their hands to themselves. But their temporary truce soon becomes a temporary tryst!

#2534 TEMPTED BY THE WRONG TWIN
Texas Cattleman's Club: Blackmail • by Rachel Bailey

Harper Lake is pregnant, but the father isn't who she thinks—it's her boss's identical twin brother! Wealthy former Navy SEAL Nick Tate pretended to be his brother as a favor, and now he's proposing a marriage of convenience that just might lead to real romance...

#2535 THE TEXAN'S BABY PROPOSAL
Callahan's Clan • by Sara Orwig

Millionaire Texan Marc Medina must marry immediately to inherit his grandfather's ranch. When his newly single secretary tells him she's pregnant, he knows a brilliant deal when he sees one. He'll make her his wife...and have her in his bed!

#2536 LITTLE SECRETS: CLAIMING HIS PREGNANT BRIDE by Sarah M. Anderson

Restless—that's businessman and biker Seth Bolton. But when he rescues pregnant runaway bride Kate Burroughs, he wants much more than he should with the lush mom-to-be... But she won't settle for anything less than taming his heart!

#2537 FROM TEMPTATION TO TWINS
Whiskey Bay Brides • by Barbara Dunlop

When Juliet Parker goes home to reopen her grandfather's restaurant, she clashes with her childhood crush, tycoon Caleb Watford, who's building a rival restaurant. Then the stakes skyrocket after their one night leaves her expecting two little surprises!

#2538 THE TYCOON'S FIANCÉE DEAL
The Wild Caruthers Bachelors • by Katherine Garbera

Derek Caruthers promised his best friend that their fake engagement would end after he'd secured his promotion...but what's a man of honor to do when their red-hot kisses prove she's the only one for him?

Get 2 Free Books,
Plus 2 Free Gifts—
just for trying the Reader Service!

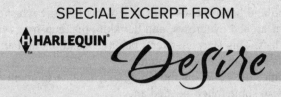
Why Linc had ever agreed to meet with his ex-fiancée's
sister was confounding. But he'd heard something in her
voice, a note of panic and sorrow. Maybe something had
happened to Kari, and, if so, he needed to know what.
She was still his son's mother, after all.

Linc heard the light rap on the door and sucked in a
breath.

His first thought when he opened his front door to Tate
Harper was that he wanted her. Under him, on top of him,
up against the nearest wall…any way he could have her.

That thought was immediately followed by *Oh, crap,
not again.*

He knew the Harpers were trouble. Kari had been a
stunning woman, but her beauty, as he knew—and paid
for—had taken work. The woman standing behind the
stroller was effortlessly gorgeous. Her hair was a riot of

blond and brown, eyes the color of his favorite whiskey under arched eyebrows, and her skin, makeup-free, was flawless. This Harper sister's beauty was all natural and, dammit, so much more potent.

Linc, his hand on the doorknob, took a moment to draw in some much-needed air.

"Tate? Come on in."

She pushed the stroller into the hall with a white-knuckled grip. Linc, wincing at the realization that he was allowing a whole bunch of trouble to walk through his front door, was about to rescind his invitation. Then he made the mistake of looking into her eyes.

She'd jumped into the ring with Kari and had the crap kicked out of her, Linc realized. And, for some reason, she thought he could help her clean up the mess. And because his first instinct was to protect, to make things right, he wanted to wipe the fear from Tate's expression.

Linc closed his eyes and reminded himself to start using his brain.

He needed to hear Tate's story so he could hustle her out the door and get back to his predictable, safe, sensible world. She was pure temptation, and being attracted to his crazy ex's sister was a complication he most definitely did not need.

Don't miss
THE CEO'S NANNY AFFAIR
by Joss Wood, available August 2017 wherever
Harlequin® Desire books and ebooks are sold.

www.Harlequin.com

LOVE
Harlequin
romance?

Join our Harlequin community to share your thoughts and connect with other romance readers!

Be the first to find out about promotions, news, and exclusive content!

Sign up for the Harlequin e-newsletter and download a free book from any series at **www.TryHarlequin.com**

CONNECT WITH US AT:

Harlequin.com/Community

 Facebook.com/HarlequinBooks

Twitter.com/HarlequinBooks

Instagram.com/HarlequinBooks

Pinterest.com/HarlequinBooks

ReaderService.com

**ROMANCE WHEN
YOU NEED IT**

HSOCIAL2017

EXCLUSIVE LIMITED TIME OFFER AT
www.HARLEQUIN.com

$7.99 U.S./$9.99 CAN.

$1.⁰⁰ OFF

New York Times Bestselling Author
MAISEY YATES

returns with a brand-new sweet and sexy tale about a Texas cowboy who comes home to Copper Ridge to put down roots in

Down Home
Cowboy

Available June 27, 2017
Get your copy today!

Receive **$1.00 OFF** the purchase price of
DOWN HOME COWBOY by Maisey Yates
when you use the coupon code below on Harlequin.com.

DOWNHOME1

Offer valid from June 27, 2017, until July 31, 2017, on www.Harlequin.com.

Valid in the U.S.A. and Canada only. To redeem this offer, please add the print or ebook version of DOWN HOME COWBOY by Maisey Yates to your shopping cart and then enter the coupon code at checkout.

HQN™
www.HQNBooks.com

PHCOUPMYHD0717